How My Summer Went Up in Flames

How My Summer Went Up in Flames

JENNIFER SALVATO DOKTORSKI

SIMON PULSE

NEW YORK LONDON TORONTO SYDNEY NEW DELHI

SIMON PULSE

An imprint of Simon & Schuster Children's Publishing Division

1230 Avenue of the Americas, New York, NY 10020

First Simon Pulse edition May 2013

Copyright © 2013 by Jennifer Salvato Doktorski

All rights reserved, including the right of reproduction in whole or in part in any form.

SIMON PULSE and colophon are registered trademarks of Simon & Schuster, Inc.

For information about special discounts for bulk purchases,

please contact Simon & Schuster Special Sales at

1-866-506-1949 or business@simonandschuster.com.

The Simon & Schuster Speakers Bureau can bring authors to your live event.

For more information or to book an event contact the

Simon & Schuster Speakers Bureau at 1-866-248-3049 or

visit our website at www.simonspeakers.com.

Designed by Karina Granda

The text of this book was set in Adobe Caslon Pro.

Manufactured in the United States of America

2 4 6 8 10 9 7 5 3 1

Library of Congress Cataloging-in-Publication Data

Doktorski, Jennifer Salvato.

How my summer went up in flames / Jennifer Salvato Doktorski. — 1st Simon Pulse ed.

p. cm.

Summary: Placed under a temporary retraining order for torching her former boyfriend's car, seventeen-year-old Rosie embarks on a cross-country car trip from New Jersey to Arizona while waiting for her court appearance.

[1. Voyages and travels—Fiction. 2. Love—Fiction. 3. Friendship—Fiction. 4. Justice, Administration of—Fiction.] I. Title.

PZ7.D69744How 2013

[Fic]—dc23

2012019019

ISBN 978-1-4424-5940-3 (hc)

ISBN 978-1-4424-5939-7 (pbk)

ISBN 978-1-4424-5941-0 (eBook)

For my parents,

Grace and George Salvato.

Thank you for a lifetime of

love, support, and family adventures.

I love you.

How My
Summer
Went Up
in Flames

Chapter 1

I wasn't always the kind of girl who wakes up on the first day of summer vacation to find herself on the receiving end of a temporary restraining order. But things got ugly when Joey, my ex, came to an end-of-the-school-year party on Friday night with his new girlfriend—the bleach-blond freshman ho bag he'd been cheating on me with. Until I saw them together, I didn't know he and his indiscretion had become an actual item. It felt like someone had knocked all the air out of my lungs with a blunt object. What can I say? First I lost my heart. Then I lost my mind.

I stare out the screen door and watch as the patrol car drives away, my face burning with embarrassment. What if Mrs. Friedman is watching from across the street? She doesn't miss a thing, ever. What a crappy start to a Monday morning.

"This cannot be happening," I say.

"Rosie, you blew up your boyfriend's car. What did you expect?" says Matty, our next-door neighbor.

"For the last time, I did not blow up Joey's car. It caught fire!"

"What's the difference?"

"Hello, there was no explosion. I was just burning all the stuff he gave me in his driveway." Why doesn't anyone understand this? I've spent all weekend trying to explain it. "The box wasn't even near Joey's car. He was standing right there. I don't know how it happened."

"Lighter fluid and stuffed animals. Bad combination," Matty says.

"Shut up, Matty! I need to think."

"The thinking ship sailed when you lit that match."

"It was a lighter and—what are you doing in my house, anyway?" It's like he doesn't even pretend to go home anymore. When Matty was six, my mother offered to let him come over after school so his mom didn't have to pay for child care. Apparently Matty thought that meant forever.

Matty extricates himself from the couch and walks

toward the front door, where I've been rendered immobile by this latest turn of events. "Take it easy, all right? I'm not the problem, your bad temper is."

"I don't have a bad temper." I look down at my purple toenails, away from Matty's beady blue-eyed stare. "I'm passionate."

"Call it whatever makes you feel better. I've grown immune to your acerbic wit and biting sarcasm, but lately it's like you're . . . I don't know, hostile?"

Hostile? Where does he get hostile? Okay. Maybe I'm high-strung. I'll give him that. But at our house, we yell when we're happy, we yell when we're upset, we yell when we want someone to pass the remote. It's what we Catalanos do.

I look down at the paper in my hand. "I guess Joey must've called the cops."

"Ya think?"

I feel like I've just done a belly flop on dry land. My parents are going to freak. They already grounded me, indefinitely, after Joey's mom called Saturday morning to scream about the postparty car fire caused by yours truly. And now there's a restraining order. At this point, my parents will lock me in a tower until I graduate from high school next

June. For a brief second I wonder if I can keep the whole thing a secret. Yeah, right, like that'll ever work. I couldn't even burn a box of memories without the police getting involved. I don't know what's happening with me lately.

"Maybe it's a mistake," I say.

Matty grabs the three-page document from me. "Right. This is for the other Rosalita Ariana Catalano Joey dated, who also blew up his car."

I cross my arms and scowl as Matty scans the page. "I've got to talk to him."

"You're to stay away from Joey's house, his job. There's to be no written, personal, or electronic communication with the complaining witness by you or anyone you know." He pauses. "It actually says you are prohibited from returning to the scene of the violence."

"I've got to talk to him," I repeat.

"Have you been listening?" Matty waves the papers in my face. "Restraining order."

"But if I can just explain—"

"Save it for your court date in two weeks."

"What?" Court date? I snatch the papers from him and start flipping through the pages, but my eyes won't settle on any words. Fruity Pebbles rise in my throat and I start to sweat. I suddenly want to throw something at the TV screen. *The View* is on—leave it to Matty. Now I have the urge to throw something at the whiny one's head. Maybe I do have anger issues.

I hand the TRO back to Matty. "I can't find it."

"Right here," he says, pointing to the correct page. "You've been ordered to appear before Superior Court Judge Tomlinson in Essex County, New Jersey, to address the allegations of, let's see, criminal trespass, criminal mischief, harassment, and stalking. Stalking?"

I cover my eyes with both hands. I think I'm either going to vomit or cry. At the moment, I can't decide which would make me feel better. I part my fingers to look at Matty. "It was only a few e-mails and texts."

"A few?"

"And maybe I showed up at ShopRite once or twice when he was getting off work."

"Good way to keep busy after a breakup. Hoping incarceration would fill those empty hours?" Matty says.

He looks as pained as I feel, which is why I need food. I walk into the kitchen and begin opening cabinets in search of the perfect snack to calm me down. Let's see. Temporary restraining order . . . I bypass the pretzels and head straight for the Double Stuf Oreos. I tear open the new package, which rouses Pony, our ninety-pound Lab mix, who'd been sleeping under the kitchen's central-air duct. I smile when he turns his head quizzically as if to say, "Did I hear food?"

"Some watchdog," I say in the baby-talk voice I use when speaking to my pooch and for which Eddie, my brother, always makes fun of me. "Where were you ten minutes ago when the police were at the door? Cookies are a different story, huh?"

Pony saunters over to the counter and nudges my elbow with his big wet nose until I relent. Sugary foods are bad for dogs, but I can't resist his pleading eyes. "Only one, big guy," I say. He gently takes the Oreo and swallows it in a single gulp. Matty comes into the kitchen just as I'm about to pour myself some milk.

"I think I know how to handle this," he says.

Matty is always trying to handle things. Most of the time, it makes me sad that he thinks he has to. I blame his absent father, not that Matty and I ever talk about him. Still, I know one of the reasons Matty likes hanging out at our house so much is that he gets to be a kid here. At sixteen, Matty is a year younger than me, the same age as my brother, and at least a foot taller than us both. When I was in middle school, Eddie and I finally stopped arguing about who Matty "belonged" to. He's our Matty. I love him like a second brother, and unfortunately, sometimes I fight with him like he's one too.

Lately, most of our spats are my fault. I know I've been impossible to be around since just after Memorial Day weekend. That's when I went away with my family and Joey cheated on me with the freshman slut. To his credit, he told me. He begged me to forgive him. He said all they did was kiss. That it was a huge mistake, a onetime thing, blah, blah, blah. As much as I wanted to believe him, I was hurt, angry, and completely shocked. I couldn't get over it and consequently, my entire relationship imploded. Since then, if I didn't know me, I'd think I was a bitch too. And that's why at this moment especially, it's best if Matty leaves. I don't want to cause an argument.

"I'm gonna call my girls," I say. "Wait until they hear this." My best friend, Lilliana, and the rest of our group will understand. I wasn't stalking Joey—right? I honestly don't know what I thought I was doing. Looking for evidence that Joey's fling was a one-night stand? Hoping to find him moping around town wearing an I ♥ ROSIE T-shirt? Whatever it was, I certainly didn't think it was illegal. If only it hadn't culminated in an accidental car fire.

I swallow my last bite of Oreo and start dialing. Matty takes my phone from me.

"I think you need to get out of town for a while," he says.

I grab my phone back. "I think you need to get out of my house for a while."

"I'm serious. I'm leaving for Arizona on Saturday with Spencer and Logan. You should come."

Okay. Here's where my curiosity trumps my need for him to go home. "Who are Spencer and Logan?"

I know some of Matty's friends, but not all. Matty goes to public school, the same school as my ex and his new chicken-head girlfriend. Oh, and my brother, Eddie, of course. My parents thought it was best for me to attend an all-girls Catholic high school because it's every teen-age girl's dream to dress like a Scottish bagpipe player. All because I got busted at an eighth-grade graduation party playing seven minutes in heaven with Armand DelVecchio, who, by the way, kisses like a seal. It wasn't even worth it.

"Spencer Davidson. We're in robotics club together."

"No surprise there."

"Logan's his older brother. He got accepted to ASU."

"Okaay, so why's he leaving now?"

"He has to be there for this special summer session. Logan wants his car in Tempe, so he figured he'd make a road trip out of it. Me and Spence are flying home."

Has Matty told me all this before? Did the information get lost in my I-just-broke-up-with-my-boyfriend haze? I'm feeling a bit guilty.

"So, why did Spencer ask you to go?"

"He's afraid to fly."

Of course he is. So now I'm picturing the scene: me, trapped in a car with three nerds. Doubtful. "And I should go because—"

"It will keep you out of trouble for nine days. You can't stalk anyone in New Jersey while traveling seventy-five miles per hour in a vehicle headed west."

I pretend to think about this for a second. "Right. Sure, I'll go."

"Really?"

"No."

After filling in Lilliana on the whole restraining-order ordeal, I spend the rest of the day trying to distract myself, which is what I've been trying to do every day since Joey and I broke up. Today, it got a lot harder. I take Pony for a long walk before attempting to read one of my romance novels. Usually I plow through them to get to the happy ending, but today, only five pages in, I toss the book aside. Lately, everything—books, song lyrics, movies, even Yankee games—reminds me of Joey.

Eventually, I settle for mindless eating and cable TV. I just want to feel normal again. I love, love, love those shows where they help women find wedding dresses. The gowns are so gorgeous, and I always seem to know which dress the bride-to-be is going to pick. That inspired me to get a part-time summer job at Something New Bridal Boutique downtown. I start next weekend and I cannot wait. I've got a definite knack for knowing what people look good in and think I have untapped potential for designing clothes. I smile as I remember this fashion studio drawing set I had when I was a kid. It had a light board, colored pencils, and all these traceable patterns. I spent hours mixing and matching the templates for tops and bottoms, hairdos and shoes, to create my own sketches. I kept my designs in a folder. My mom, who used to pretend to be a client, wrote ROSIE COUTURE on it for me. I wonder if I still have that folder somewhere.

Around three in the afternoon, I decide to lay out on the deck. The whole world just seems better when I'm tan. I love how my skin smells after I come in from the sun. Pony whines to come outside with me—he always follows me around when I'm home. But after five minutes, he starts panting and stands by the back door.

That's when I remember I forgot to put on sunscreen. I get up to let him in, find a bottle in the kitchen cabinet, and return to the deck. My olive skin is immune to sunburn, but I'm paranoid about skin cancer and premature wrinkling. As soon as I open the bottle, I wish that I had risked it and done without my SPF 50. The tropical scent immediately takes me back to the first time I saw Joey. He was standing on the boardwalk near the pirate-themed mini-golf course. It was September, a warm Indian summer day, and me and Lilliana'd crammed in one last beach day. I was balancing on one foot, dusting the sand off my toes so I could put my flip-flop back on, when I spotted him. He caught me staring, but I never even had a chance to be embarrassed.

"I've seen you before," he said. I couldn't believe this beautiful boy was talking to me. "Your brother goes to Chestnutville High, doesn't he?" I was totally self-conscious because my long hair was all frizzy after a day of sun and salt water. I tried to casually smooth it down while I talked to him, but then he reached over and brushed a stray ringlet away from my eye, like he was already used to invading my personal space, and said: "I love your curls."

A week later, we were a couple.

I think about our first date a lot, remembering how I watched from my bedroom window as he pulled into the driveway. I had been ready for an hour, but I figured I'd let Joey ring the bell and sweat out the first meeting with my family before I went downstairs. If he was going to be a keeper, my family needed to like him and he needed to like my family.

I stood on the upstairs landing, out of sight, and listened to the introductions, followed by easy laughter when my brother said, "There's still time to back out, man. I don't think Rosie knows you're here." When I walked down the stairs a few seconds later wearing a yellow silk tank top that contrasted nicely with my dark eyes and hair (I had worn it curly for him), I could tell he had no intention of bailing. He was all in. Neither of us said a word, but we were both smiling like it was yearbook picture day. People think those time-stands-still moments only happen in movies. They don't. It sounds cheesy, but everyone else just faded away and it felt like we were alone.

"Do you two know each other?" my dad said, breaking the spell. Everyone laughed and then we walked out the door.

As Joey opened the car door for me, he leaned down and whispered in my ear: "You're even prettier than I remembered." A chill rippled from my neck and spread across my body.

Before my date, Matty and Eddie did try to warn me that Joey had a love-'em-and-leave-'em rep around school. But that night, Joey seemed more like an anxious little boy than some arrogant Casanova. He asked me a ton of questions and wanted to know everything about me. It was like I really, really mattered. And he seemed so worried about whether or not I was enjoying myself. I lost count of how many times he asked if my tortellini with pesto sauce was any good. When he spilled his water and his entire face turned red, my heart went out to him. I was making him nervous. Me. I didn't care what Eddie and Matty said about how Joey treated girls in the past. I could tell I was going to be different.

Ha! What a joke. I put the cap back on my sunscreen, lie down, and close my eyes. Forget it. I already got burned.

* * *

At five o'clock, I change back into shorts and a tank top and brace myself for what's coming. At dinner, the tiny lift I got from a healthy dose of vitamin D is gone. Probably because we're having pork cutlets and salad with a heated family discussion about criminal mischief on the side.

"Say that again, Rosie," Mom says. "It sounded like you said 'restraining order.'"

"I did. 'Temporary restraining order.'"

I hold out the document halfheartedly. My mother takes it from me, stares at it, closes her eyes, and passes it to my father.

"Oh, *Dios mío*," Mom says. "Are you trying to kill your father and me? This business with Joey keeps getting worse."

Here we go with the Spanglish. Worrying always transforms my mom into George Lopez. Predictably, the veins in my dad's neck bulge out as he reads the restraining order. Let's hope he doesn't transform into the Incredible Hulk.

"I don't know you anymore," Dad says. He's got the papers rolled up and waves them around like a light saber. "My daughter would never do these things."

Well, your daughter did, apparently, says the Rosie in my head. He's right, though. I hate to disappoint my dad. I pick at my food as he gets up and starts pacing. I waited until after he ate to tell everyone. Low blood sugar tends to fuel my father's anger. My mother just rubs her temples. Pony, who had been under the table waiting for scraps, slinks out of the room. Smart dog.

"I'd better not find out you slept with this boy," my father shouts.

"Oh my God, Dad! You did not just say that." I cover my ears. Eddie looks mortified. So does Mom.

That's when Matty materializes at the back door. I spot him first and can tell he's afraid to knock. I'm guessing he's waiting for a pause in my dad's tirade. Finally, Matty taps on the door. His arrival is a welcome diversion—my parents adore Matty.

"Sorry to interrupt," Matty says. "Did Rosie tell you about my plan?"

Wait, what? Why would I? I had practically forgotten until this very second that he'd gone all road trip on me. Okay, maybe Matty isn't a good diversion, but it's too late, he's already pulling up a chair. So, ten minutes later, after he shares his whole getting-out-of-Dodge scheme (he actually calls it that), my parents have fallen into an eerie trance.

"Let me get this straight," Eddie says. "Rosie blows up a car and now she's going on vacation?"

"For the last time, it didn't blow up," I say. "And who says I even want to go?"

"Whatever," Eddie says. "Then I'm going too."

"As much as I'd like to send you along to watch out for your sister, you can't," Mom says. "You have to work."

Eddie is lifeguarding at the town pool club this summer. This is the dream job he's wanted since he was a kid and took swim lessons at the YMCA. There's no way he's giving it up. Furthermore, there's no way I'm giving up my own summer plans. I've got the bridal shop gig on weekends and I was planning on supplementing that money by starting a dog-walking-slash-sitting business. I made up flyers and everything. Plus, at the end of August, I'm supposed to spend two weeks with Lilliana and her family at their beach house.

"Rosie's not going either," Dad says.

"That's a relief," I mumble.

"She's going to work for me at the factory. That way, I can keep an eye on her."

Uh-oh. I spoke too soon. My dad runs the family lampshade business with his brother, my uncle Dominic. Oh, I've done my time at the factory, cutting lampshades into three-by-five rectangular swatches, punching holes in the corners, and grouping the fabrics on binder rings as samples. I have to admit, I've got a gift for arranging certain colors and textures so they're appealing to customers. More than samples, I create palettes.

Still, I am so over it. This summer, I wanted to try something different, even though I feel guilty for not helping Dad more. The business has taken a hit during the last few years with so much stuff being manufactured in countries like China and all, and my mom's salary as an assistant bank manager doesn't exactly make up for it. Now we've got to hire a lawyer. My parents don't need to be shelling out that kind of money right now.

It's official. I suck.

I promise myself I'll be a better daughter, just as soon as I work out this megamess with Joey. Maybe we can both say we're sorry and start over again. Is that what I want? That's part of the problem. I don't think I'll know until I talk to Joey again. What I do know is that I want this conversation to be over. I look at the clock on the microwave. Lilliana and her cousin Marissa are picking me up down the street soon. If I can sneak out, we're going to do a drive-by of Joey's house and job.

"Maybe she should go away," Mom says. She's skimming Matty's trip itinerary.

"What?!" Dad bellows. "We don't even know these boys."

"Well, of course we'll need to call their parents, and Matty will be with her," Mom says. I'm not sure I like where she's going with this.

"Look," Mom continues. "It's not my first choice either. But it will keep Rosie out of trouble until her court date, and she might learn something."

"You're not serious!" Eddie shouts. His nose and forehead are pink, and he has white circles around his eyes in the shape of his sunglasses. He really needs to get some better sunscreen—it's hard to take Raccoon Boy's anger seriously. I stifle the urge to tell him that. I'm already in enough trouble.

"Stay out of this, Eddie," Mom says. "In fact, go outside. All of you. I want to talk to your father."

Outside, I plop my butt on the cushiony chaise lounge on the deck. Matty and Eddie walk down into the yard to shoot hoops. There's a net mounted to our detached garage. It's a good thing that in addition to being Super Dork, Matty is freaking excellent at basketball. He was the only sophomore on varsity. It no doubt saves him from many an ass kicking.

I close my eyes and try to pretend it's a regular summer night. I'm kinda pissed because I'm realizing that blowing up your ex's car and getting a restraining order really robs a person of the sympathy that is her due. I would never say this out loud, but I'm not even that sorry I did it. I'm still angry and hurt. I was in love with Joey, he was my first real boyfriend, and he cheated on me. Ever since we broke up, I've been harboring hope that he was telling the truth when he said that his one-night screwup meant nothing. So when I saw him with his new girl at Kevin's party on Friday, it was like a bikini wax times ten. Even though I knew about her, I didn't think they were dating. I didn't think she could fit under his arm as well as I did. Seeing him with her . . . I came unglued.

But the really screwed-up part of all this is, I still love him. In my head, I had us married with two kids, living right here in town with the rest of my entire extended family. High school sweethearts. Happily ever after. The end. I know I'm supposed to have dreams about college and a career, but the truth is, I dream about my wedding day more. Neither of my parents went to college, and look at the life they built together. Sure, Eddie and I get on each other's nerves sometimes, but for the most part, I'm pretty lucky. My family is close and there's no question we love one another.

A car horn gives two quick beeps as it passes by the front of the house, waking me from my thoughts. I get up from the chaise and peek in through the screen door. My parents are locked in an exchange of intense whispers. I open the door and try to act super casual.

"I'm going upstairs," I say. Neither parent acknowledges me. Cool. I make a point of running loudly upstairs before creeping silently back down, carrying my flip-flops. Luckily, the front door isn't visible from the kitchen. Pony is asleep on the couch. I don't want him waking up, running to the kitchen to grab his leash, and busting me. I turn the doorknob carefully and slip out, vowing to make it the last time I do something like this. For a while, at least.

I round the corner and see Lilliana's car. She fist bumps me when I get in. "A restraining order. Nice."

Lilliana and her younger cousin Marissa go to Sacred Heart with me. We despise plaid and have a shared, but silent, contempt for authority. We've never had detention, and we get along with mostly everyone. I've noticed that girls treat each other pretty good when there are no boys around to impress. All-girl schools still have their cliques, but my friends are the nonjoiners who feel too cool for student council and Spanish club. But the trouble I'm in doesn't feel cool at all. I get light-headed every time I think about what people are saying about me. What's going to happen when school starts again? Am I going to have one of those social outcast nicknames like "Psycho Torch Girl" or something?

"Let's get the drive-by of the dirtbag's house over with," Lilliana says. "Then we're taking you out."

Lilliana is no longer hiding the fact that she never liked Joey. It's only because she missed me. Joey and I were inseparable.

"I can't go out. I'm grounded, remember?" I say. "It's bad enough I'm sneaking out to do this."

"Maybe we shouldn't go," Marissa says.

"Don't be such a wuss," Lilliana snaps.

"A restraining order is serious. Rosie can get in legal trouble if someone sees her near his house," Marissa pleads.

I feel bad for making her nervous. I'm a good girl at heart. A few months ago, I would have felt the same way. Joey cheating on me has caused me to undergo some kind of psychological shift. Sure, I can be loud and dramatic, but flat-out rebellion was never my thing.

"No one will see me. I'll hide back here, I promise," I say, slouching down in the backseat.

I sound confident, but I know I can't keep doing stuff like this. Do I really want to turn out like one of those reality-show freaks? My dad said he doesn't know me anymore. That makes two of us.

We take Farms Road, which starts on my end of town where the older-style homes are only a driveway's width apart, and wind through the small downtown area. We pass the corner deli where the skate kids are hanging out and continue on Farms until it brings us to Joey's neighborhood, where the houses are newer and larger but more cookie cutter, right down to the identical play sets in nearly every yard. A month ago, this was my favorite route. Tonight, it makes me anxious and sick. When we pull into Elm Court, I duck.

"Tell me if you see him," I say. "Is there anyone outside?"

"Nope," Lilliana says.

"Is his car there? Does it look damaged?"

"No cars in the driveway," Lilliana says. "No lights on either. It doesn't look like anyone's home."

"He's probably at work. Let's drive by ShopRite next," I say.

My phone rings while I'm still crouching down in the backseat. Shit! It's my mother. She knows I left the house. She knows I'm up to something. She knows everything. Damn the Catalano sixth sense.

"Hello?"

"Where are you?"

"I'm in Lilliana's car." This is not a lie.

"And where is Lilliana's car, Rosie?"

"It's at the diner. We're about to go inside." Of course, that is a lie.

"That's it," Mom snaps. "You're coming home right now! Your father is furious."

"I know I shouldn't have left the house, but it's just the diner and—"

"Look out the back window," Mom says. I can hear her clenching her teeth.

"Uh-oh," Lilliana says, glancing in her rearview mirror.

Slowly, I rise up off the floor and look out the back car window. Yep. There's my mom in her SUV.

"You followed me?" I shriek into the phone, which is still at my ear.

"I didn't need to. I knew where to find you."

I squint in the low, dusk light. There's someone in the passenger's seat. Dad? Eddie? No effin' way.

"Is that Matty?" It is. Traitor.

"He talked your father into staying home," Mom says. "You should be happy you've got a friend like him."

I should be, but at the moment, I'm not.

Chapter 2

I'm leaving for Arizona on Saturday. I could go into the details of the Catalano Monday Night Smackdown that led to their decision to send their only daughter on a nine-day cross-county road trip, but it's too exhausting. Suffice it to say, Mom's Ecuadorian temper, I mean passion, trumps Dad's Italian brand. Dad is loud all the time. Mom is loud when she needs to be. We never say it, but we all know Mom wears the pants in this family.

"Call your goofball friends and tell them I'm in," I say when Matty answers the phone. It's late, but I knew he'd still be up.

"Cool. I'm sorry if I got you into trouble, Rosie. I was just trying—"

"No, no. I'm the one who should be sorry. I screwed up. Again. Thanks for having my back."

"Anytime," Matty says. He sounds relieved. We should all aspire to be Mattys.

"But I need my space until Saturday, got it?"

"Got it."

"No watching *The View* on our couch."

"I got it. I got it. You're gonna thank me for this."

"Don't get carried away." I hang up.

I'm drained from the family drama, but I still can't sleep. Pony is sacked out on my twin bed anyway. He has his head on my pillow and he's making these cute mini-yelp noises while his feet twitch. Aw, poor guy. Doggy nightmare. I gently stroke the top of his head between his ears until he settles into a quiet slumber. I sigh. Maybe my dog-walking business will still work out when I get back, but who knows what will happen when I call the bridal shop tomorrow. I can't expect them to hold my job.

I grab my stuffed Clydesdale that I got from Busch Gardens when I was seven and give it a squeeze. When I was little, I had these dreams of learning to ride and begged my parents for a horse every year until my thirteenth birthday, when I got Pony. Luckily, that ten-pound bundle of chocolate-colored fur grew into his name. He was, and is, the best birthday gift ever. Still, I didn't abandon my first "horse," Clyde. How could I? I logged a lot of cuddle time with him before Pony arrived. I've still never been on a horse.

I settle into a spot on the floor between my bed and the open window and sift through my Joey Box outtakes. I didn't burn everything in the fire. There's some stuff I can't part with, like the first card he gave me and the dried, pressed rose from our one-month anniversary. Every month he gave me another. Guess I'll never get my dozen.

Then there's the picture Lilliana took of us at the winter semiformal. We're slow dancing. Joey is in a suit and tie, looking all male-model-ish with his ice-blue eyes and black hair. I look good too, not that I like to brag. It was just one of those nights when everything fell into place. Perfect hair. No zits or bloating, and I found this amazing metallic silver eyeliner that really made my brown eyes pop. I wore a black lace strapless dress that showed off my cleavage but was classy at the same time. Every inch of me felt good.

What happened to us? That was the night Joey told me he loved me for the first time. He swore I was the first girl he spoke those words to. I believed him. Still do. The

Joey Marconi in this photo picked me up every day after school and almost always brought me something that he knew I'd like—an iced coffee, Swedish fish, a Big Gulp. We spent every day together. And he told me everything. Like how he cried in first grade because the kids used to call him Joey Macaroni, how he felt like his older brothers outshined him in everything, from high school sports to the rivalry for their father's attention. My Joey said he'd never push me to take our relationship to the next level. He said he'd wait forever.

When did things change between us, and why didn't I notice? Joey cheats. We break up. He calls the cops. Maybe it was his mom's idea. She never liked me that much. Even after Joey and I had been dating for nine months, she always acted surprised to see me. She was all, "Oh, Rosie. I didn't know you were here." Or, "Oh, Rosie, I didn't realize you and Joey were going to the movies tonight." No one is good enough for her baby boy. Between Joey and his two older brothers, it's like Oedipal overload in that house.

And yet, all I want is to see Joey again. The more I'm told I can't, the more convinced I am that everything will be okay if I can just see his face and tell him why I did what I did. And give him a chance to apologize for being

a two-timing snake. Everyone makes mistakes. I can forgive him, right? Then he can forgive me. I never meant for
things to go so, so wrong.

I know I can fix this. So that's why, for the second time
in one day, I violate the terms of my TRO. The acronym
sounds better. In my head, at least. I keep my text short:
CALL ME. R. An hour later, I'm ashamed to admit, I send
another. WE NEED TO TALK. PLEASE? I fall asleep sometime
after three in the morning, still clutching my phone, my
heart breaking all over again.

His silence hurts more than his cheating.

The smell of bacon and coffee wakes me early the next
morning, despite the fact that I hardly slept, and I feel even
more depressed. All I want to do is stay in bed until my
court date is over. But my stomach growls. Is there any
better smell? There's no real cure for heartache, but bacon
comes close. My body feels heavy and my pillow is winning
the tug-of-war against those crispy strips until I reach for
my phone. It isn't on my comforter. I kick off the covers and
search the tangle of sheets and then under my bed. Gone.
Stealth mom strikes again. I haul my groggy butt downstairs in my cotton pajamas shorts and matching tee with

a picture that looks like a little Pony and says PUPPY LOVE. I'm embarrassed about those messages to Joey and afraid of Mom's reaction.

I stop abruptly at the kitchen doorway when I hear my mom talking on the phone. I know it's Dad. He calls her every morning when he gets to work, even though he left less than an hour ago. I usually admire my parents' close relationship, but this morning, I know they're talking about me. I'm hoping Dad changed his mind and doesn't want me to go to Arizona. I have to admit, the trip might help me get my mind off Joey, but does it have to be so far and with two guys I don't really know?

"Agreed," Mom says just as I step into the kitchen. "Matty's in charge." She's holding my cell. I'm totally screwed yet feeling oddly self-righteous and confrontational. I stand in front of Mom, arms crossed with my grouch face on. She gives me the "one second" motion with her pointer finger. "Uh-huh, yes. Me too. I'll talk to her when she gets up. Love you." Mom clicks off and I start in before she has a chance to.

"What do you mean, 'Matty's in charge'? I seriously hope you're not talking about me!"

"Calm down. Your father and I just don't want to see

you get into any more trouble." Mom points my phone at me while she speaks. "Your father is contacting a lawyer today. We need to find out what has to be done before this court date and make sure it's okay for you to leave the state. He's stressed enough about his business; we can't have you calling and texting Joey from here to Arizona."

"So you mean Matty is getting control of my phone?"

"Sweetie, it's for the best. We love you."

"So I'm going to be on house arrest, except in a car." I give Mom my pout face. "Keep my phone. I'll just borrow Matty's."

"You know how much I text you and your brother. I don't want to run up Matty's bill. And anyway—" Mom shakes her head.

"What?"

Her shoulders slump in resignation. "There's a GPS in your phone. Your father will feel better if we track you during this trip."

"Holy mother of . . . are you kidding me? A GPS? Since when?"

"Since always. From the time we got you your first phone."

"Eddie better have one too."

30

"Watch your tone, young lady. He does. He just doesn't know about it."

I'm certainly not going to tell him. Let him find out the hard way. Then I begin inventorying any other lies I may have told over the years regarding my physical location. It's all too much. My head is spinning.

"I can't take this. I don't want to go. Please don't make me go. Who's gonna walk Pony? You know he only likes to sleep with me."

"The dog will be fine, and you don't have a choice. Look, this isn't easy for us, either, but it's clear that you're not thinking about the consequences of your actions." Mom massages her temple and I can tell she's not done talking. "Believe it or not, I know what it's like to be obsessed with a boy. Sometimes the best cure is distance. It gives you perspective. Besides, you may even have fun. Did you ever consider that?"

Obsessed? I'm not obsessed. All I can do is scowl as I grab for my Hello Kitty mug. Kitty's polka-dotted purse is fading from too many dishwasher runs, but I still love it. I fix my coffee the way I like it: First, I put in three teaspoons of sugar. Next, a splash of hot coffee to melt the sugar. Then, lots of half-and-half. Finally, I pour the coffee until it's the exact mocha shade that I like. Light and sweet. I help myself to a big plate of bacon and scrambled eggs before thinking twice about it and sliding some back onto the griddle. I'm a big eater and I've been blessed with a metabolism that keeps up, but I've been overdoing it lately. There's a delicate balance between "curvy" and "chubby."

I slip Pony a bacon strip and he gobbles it without even chewing. I'm just about to take a bite of my eggs when Matty taps on the back door and lets himself in.

"Space, remember?" I say.

"Take it easy. I'm just dropping off the revised itinerary and then I'm gone," he says. "I printed an extra copy for your parents, too."

"What a good boy." Mom gives him a hug. Inside, I'm rolling my eyes.

I'm about to say something snarky, but I just can't. With his cropped hair and perpetually flushed cheeks, no matter how old Matty gets, he's still the little boy next door.

"Thanks, Matty," I say instead.

"You're welcome," he says. "It's going to be an adventure."

I don't want an adventure. I want Joey and my old life back. But Mom and Matty are both looking at me, so I give them my best attempt at a sincere smile. I'm tired of letting people down.

* * *

The next day, I'm more shocked than anyone when my parents allow me to go to the mall with Lilliana to buy a few things for my trip. Inside, they're softies. Not that I'm gonna point this out or anything. I have to call them from the house phone both before I leave and as soon as I return. I have exactly two hours. Mom takes my cell to work with her. She considered letting Lilliana carry it—the GPS would allow her to track me all day—but she decided against it. My parents are softies, not stupid. Anyway, they don't have anything to worry about. I want to earn back their trust.

"What are you complaining about?" Lilliana asks. We're at Macy's and she's trying on sunglasses. She has an adorable button nose, the kind you'd ask for if you were getting a nose job. All styles of shades look good on her. "Three guys, the open road, Arizona. And time away from that tool. It's like a country song."

"I hate country music."

"The crossover stuff is okay."

I shrug. "I guess, but that straight-up cowboy music gets on my nerves."

"Joey gets on my nerves," Lilliana blurts out before

33

recovering her "happy face" and attempting to put a positive spin on my trip. "Maybe you'll finally go horseback riding. You've always wanted to do that," she says. "Or use the time away to get your head together. Bring a notebook. Write down your thoughts."

Thoughts? Where is this coming from? I'm not one for extracurricular thinking. Neither is she. At least I read romance novels; Lilliana's reading is restricted to whatever can be viewed on her phone.

"I'm more of an action person," I say. "I need to stay here and straighten things out with Joey."

"That's what you think you need. But let's put your effed-up feelings about Joey aside. Aren't you forgetting the bigger issue here?"

"Please don't remind me about the thing."

"Temporary restraining order? I'm just sayin'. You'll go crazy sitting around waiting for your court date. Remember what your attorney told your parents?"

"The farther away the better," I mumble. Actually his exacts words were "out-of-state equals good."

The lawyer's right. Lilliana's right. Everyone's right. And I'm cranky. I need a pick-me-up.

"Let's go to the pet store."

Just Pets sells just that. Hamsters, fish, geckos, birds—small critters. But they also have dog and puppy adoptions, so I stop by whenever I'm at the mall. I'd love a second dog, but I wouldn't want to upset Pony. He thinks he's my baby. Anyway, I'm in no position to be asking for anything right now.

Just Pets has an adorable fox terrier mix available for adoption. He's got a mostly white face with a black and brown patch over one eye. I want so badly to hold him for a few minutes, but I can't get his hopes up only to send him back. Even at a distance he's got me grinning like a fool and Lilliana has to drag me away from his crate.

"I'm getting hungry," Lilliana whines. "Let's get some shopping done before lunch."

"Okay, okay. I'm coming."

"What are we looking for exactly?" Lilliana asks as we walk toward Nordstrom's.

"Anything that will look cute after sitting in a car for hours."

"Wrinkle free. Check," Lilliana says.

"And light," I say. "Do you know Arizona is, like, a hundred and seven degrees this time of year? Literally. Is that crazy or what?"

"Your parents are sending you to hell. Hell with no ocean." Lilliana then seems to remember she's been trying to make me feel better about this road trip and attempts to smooth over her snarkiness. "But you'll probably get to see the Grand Canyon, right? Or will you? Where exactly are you going, anyway?"

I look at Lilliana and raise my eyebrows. The deeper meaning is not lost on me. On a more literal level, I know where we start and where we finish, but what about that whole middle part? It dawns on me that I have no idea. I'm still in denial that this is happening. I meant to read Matty's updated itinerary, but every time I think about it, it just makes me tired.

The shopping trip is going well; I buy some really cute shorts, tank tops, and sandals. Clothes and accessories make me feel better. I maximize my dollars by picking items that can be mixed and matched easily.

We're about to stop for lunch in the food court when we see him. He's holding hands with that bleached-out thing he calls a girlfriend, and they're standing in line at the new juice bar. Lilliana stops mid-sentence and follows my gaze.

"Rosie," she says, clutching my right arm with both

her hands. I'm not sure if she's steadying me or holding me back.

Joey doesn't see me, but the ho does, and when our eyes meet, she gives me this smirk and kisses him right on the lips—for a while. Oh really now? She must mistake me for someone with patience. She shoots me another look, prompting Joey to turn in my direction. Our eyes lock and I hate myself, but I get that hopeful flutter in my chest. He opens his mouth like he's going to say something, then puts his arm around Blondie and drags her away.

"How many feet are between me and that a-hole right now?" I ask. I move to follow them, but Lilliana digs her nails into my arm. In that moment, I am so freaking glad I blew up his car that if I hadn't already done it, I'd be in his driveway with a gas can and a lighter.

"Come on," Lilliana says, and steers me toward the exit. "We're out of here."

Neither of us speaks until we get to the car. I sit in the passenger seat, my heart pumping like a double-kick drum. My skin feels hot. The rapid rise and fall of emotions makes me dizzy. I go from anger to sadness to resignation. My parents and Matty are right. I can't risk seeing him again before my court date.

"Are you okay?" Lilliana finally asks.

I take a deep breath and wait for my pulse to slow down. My new role as Joey's crazy ex-girlfriend is anxiety inducing, depressing, and exhausting.

"I'm not sure if I'm okay, but I will be." I find a good song on the radio and turn it all the way up. "I'm leaving for Arizona in three days and I cannot wait."

Maybe saying it out loud will convince me it's true.

Chapter 3

On Saturday morning, I follow Matty and Eddie onto the front porch and into the predawn darkness. I'm feeling extra groggy because I had a hard time getting to sleep and wound up taking two teaspoons of Benadryl around two in the morning. It should have knocked me out, but instead I tossed and turned like I had a fever. I even dreamed I wandered around the house looking for my phone and sent Joey a message telling him to meet me in Phoenix on the Fourth of July. Thankfully, when I woke up, my phone was nowhere in sight. My parents probably have it in a lockbox somewhere until it's time to transfer it to Matty. It felt so real, though. Craziness.

I walk down the steps and cross the lawn. The grass is wet with that annoying early-morning dew, which is making me sorry I wore flip-flops. The cicadas are chirping away and, wait . . . is that an owl? My parents follow us. Dad carries my bags; Mom clutches her coffee mug. She and I share a serious caffeine addiction. This morning, however, my stomach has that sickish first-day-of-school feeling, made worse by my antihistamine hangover. I would have thrown up if I drank or ate anything. Pony was disappointed. He knows I'm the one most likely to share my breakfast with him.

It takes me a second to realize that the burgundy Taurus in Matty's driveway is my ride. Could there be a less cool vehicle? It screams rental, not road trip. I'm still getting over the lame car when a guy gets out of the front seat and walks toward us in a Snoopy T-shirt that says PARTY LIKE A ROCK STAR. Oh, man.

"Hi, I'm Spencer," he says. No kidding.

Matty's mom walks toward us with a thin, dark-haired woman who I'm assuming is Spencer and Logan's mom. I notice a forest-green Jeep at the curb that must belong to her. Now, that's a road-trip-worthy ride. Spencer shakes everyone's hand and Mrs. Davidson introduces herself as well. Except for several lengthy phone conversations between my mom and theirs (and probably a background check performed on the sly by one of my father's state trooper buddies), this is the first time we're all meeting. My parents are all smiles. Oh, I can read their minds all right. They're thinking, *Hallelujah! Rosie is going to Arizona with Matty and a member of the Peanuts gang. What could possibly go wrong?* But then Logan, the answer to my parents' silent, rhetorical question, gets out of the car. He's wearing perfect-fitting jeans and a dark gray V-neck shirt. The short sleeves hug his biceps, which appear perpetually flexed. His torso is twice the size of Spencer's, and he's sporting a sexy five o'clock shadow that would take Matty three weeks to grow. I'm suddenly angry at myself for not bothering with mascara and eyeliner and fumble in my bag for my shades, even though the sun has yet to break the horizon. Thankfully, I did my hair. I always do my hair.

"I'm Logan," he says. *Yes. Yes, you are!* I'm thinking as he shakes everyone's hand.

"Don't worry. We'll take good care of Rosie." Logan smiles at my parents and then me, and I notice that he's taller than all of us, even Matty.

It's like my heart rate and hormones heard the crack of the starting gun, and they're off! *No, no, no,* I tell them. *You two have gotten me in enough trouble already.* But it feels good to temporarily not have Joey in my head.

41

I look back toward our front door. Pony is watching me through the glass. He wags his tail wildly and gives me his I-need-some-lovin' face.

"Eddie, can you let Pony out? I want to say good-bye one more time."

He grumbles but does it anyway. He'd never admit it, but I know he's going to miss me. The fact that he's even awake right now speaks volumes.

As soon as Eddie opens the door, Pony bolts toward me. I think he's going to jump up on me for one last kiss, but he runs right by and goes to meet Spencer and Logan, twirling his tail like a baton. I should have known. He loves to greet new people, and it's not like he understands he won't be seeing me for a while. I try not to be jealous when Logan crouches down to pet him and Pony practically sits in his lap.

"Come 'ere, boy," I say. He obeys, and when I bend down to give him a squeeze, my chest tightens. "Make sure Eddie remembers to take you on long walks." I turn toward Eddie. "He likes to visit his pal, Suzie. She lives on Cook Road."

I give Dad a kiss on the cheek and he puts his arm around my shoulders for a sideways squeeze. He hands Matty my phone, the sight of which makes my heart double pump as I remember my texting dream. It was a dream, wasn't it?

Mom puts her empty mug down on the steps and envelops me in a big, squishy embrace. No matter how old I am, I never get tired of Mom's hugs, especially ones that leave my shirt with the lingering scent of her Estée Lauder moisturizer.

"Be good. Have fun," she says. I know without looking that she has tears in her eyes. My throat constricts.

"I will, Mom." I want it to be the truth. If not for myself, then at least for her and Dad.

"I love you."

"I love you too, Mom."

"Call us later today," Dad says.

Matty carries my bags to the car and Eddie follows. While Matty loads my stuff in the trunk, Eddie opens the door for me. Before I get in, he gives me a lightning-fast hug and whispers in my ear, "Be safe. Try not to kiss anyone."

I decide to do him a solid. "FYI. Your phone has a GPS," I whisper back. "Don't tell the parents I told you."

Eddie nods slowly as the information seeps in, and then he's gone. Logan and Spencer are already in the front seat. I'm about to sit down when I notice that Matty and I will be traveling with an acoustic guitar between us.

"Can't we put this in the trunk?" I ask.

"Logan says it takes up too much room," Spencer explains.

"So what? We can't crowd the luggage, but it's okay to crowd humans?" I ask.

My backpack is bulging with all my important stuff (e.g., credit card for emergencies, makeup, round brush, *CosmoGirl*, romance novel, Cheez-Its, and tunes) and I was hoping for more space back here.

"Just shut the door," mumbles Matty.

"Matty, can I see my phone for a sec?"

"We're still in the driveway."

"I know. Real quick. Please?" I need to put my fears to rest.

"Here." He slips it to me like it's some illicit substance.

Quickly, I page to my text messages and make sure there are none from last night. Phew. Nothing to Joey about the Fourth of July or anything else. I toss the phone back to Matty.

I wave to my family and the boys wave to their moms. As we pull out of the driveway, I'm surprised by how choked up I get. I've never been away from home before. I mean, sure, I've slept over at friends' houses and at my grandparents', and I've gone down the shore to Lilliana's family beach house, but never this far and with people I just met. My eyes fill with tears. Who gets homesick before they even leave their block? I don't have much time to dwell on this, because as soon as we turn the corner and my house is out of sight, Logan starts laying down ground rules.

"Just so you know, you're not getting any special treatment. We're going to say and do what we want, no apologies for guy behavior," Logan says.

"Fine," I tell Logan as I dig through my bag for a tissue to wipe dried grass clippings off my toes. Stupid dew. "If that includes noxious emissions, open a window. Even my little brother has the decency to do that."

"Only if we feel like it," Spencer pipes up.

Whoa, look at Snoopy growing a set of you-know-whats over there.

"Oh, yeah, and you're on our schedule," Logan continues. "No extra time for whatever girl things you've got going on. If you're not in the car when it's time to leave, we'll go without you."

"No, we won't," Matty says.

"No?" Logan looks at us in the rearview mirror, eyebrows raised. "Watch me."

"Watch me," I mimic. Mr. Tough Guy in a Taurus. My heart rate and hormones stop so fast they kick up a cloud of dust. He's one of those people who announces that he's "type A" as if it gives him permission to call the shots. I'm gonna wind up telling him what that "A" stands for before this trip is over. I can tell.

"That reminds me," Spencer says. "Here's your copy of the itinerary. It will help you stay on schedule." Another one? He hands me a double-pocket folder. Is he serious? There are maps on one side and at least ten typed pages of information on the other. He also has a contact list with all our cell phone numbers. Like we're going to get separated? I can see why he and Matty are such good friends—they're like obsessive-compulsive AAA buddies. I'm too tired to read this right now. Logan is fiddling with the radio and lands on a station that's playing country music. Nooo! Who knew we even had a country music station in the Tri-State Area?

"I don't suppose I get a vote about music," I say.

"Now you're catching on," Logan says.

I want to smack the smirk off that gorgeous face. Instead, I get my own tunes out of my backpack, put on my headphones, and close my eyes. It's my road trip too, and Springsteen is in order. Even though he's not who my friends listen to, I feel a special connection to him—even beyond the whole New Jersey thing—because my parents named me after one of his songs.

I cue up my Bruce playlist, and when the intro to "Girls in Their Summer Clothes" fills my ears, I feel a pang as I realize it's summer and I want to be at the beach, not heading two thousand miles in the wrong direction. I need to sleep. Maybe in a few hundred miles I'll look back on this, and just like it did for the Rosie in the Bruce song, it will all seem funny.

I wake up two hours later, my head against the window, the guitar's neck in my lap, and drool in the corner of my mouth. The car is parked and I'm alone. I look out the window. We're at some place called the Waffle House, and those bastards are going in without me. I push the guitar off me, wipe the spit off my face, and pick through the tangles in my long brown hair. I open the car door, grab my backpack, and stomp into the restaurant.

"Thanks a lot," I say. The three of them are standing inside the door by the sign that says PLEASE WAIT TO BE SEATED.

"We'd have woken you up by the time we were ready to order," Matty says. I'm pissed. He's the one who wanted me here, and now he's trying to starve me so he can impress Logan.

"Speak for yourself," Logan says. "She knows the rules."

Jerk. We follow the hostess to a booth by the window. I

roll my eyes at Logan and then take the window seat. Matty slides in next to me. Thankfully, I'm across from Spencer, not Logan. I might have a muscle spasm and "accidentally" kick him.

"I would have brought you a bagel or something," Spencer says. He shrugs and opens the menu.

"Thank you." I give Spencer the best smile I'm capable of without lip gloss and nudge Matty's leg with my foot. "Where are we, anyway?"

"It's on the schedule," Spencer says. "Didn't you read your itinerary?"

Sleeping, duh. But I need Spence on my side if I expect to get fed on this road trip to hell. Besides, there's no reason that Snoopy shirt should keep us from becoming friends.

"You planned all our pit stops?"

"Of course," Spencer says. "We have an aggressive schedule. I want to make sure we get to see everything we want to see."

"What if there's something I want to see?"

"Is there something you want to see, Rosie?" Matty asks.

"I dunno," I say. "I didn't have a chance to think about it."

"I guess launching a full-out vendetta against your ex-boyfriend takes up a lot of free time," Logan says.

"What's your problem?" I say. "Can't you be nice?"

He's smiling, in a cute-ish, not smirky way, and his voice softens. "I thought I was. I let you in my car, didn't I? And I haven't even asked you for gas money yet."

"I guess that begs the question, why did you let me come along, anyway?"

"Because your friend Matty said—"

A waitress in a 1950s-style uniform arrives at our table and renders Logan, and the rest of us, speechless. The woman is older than my mom and has what appears to be a black plastic tarantula in her hair.

"Are you ready to order, or do you need a few minutes?" she asks.

I'd like to order, but my brain is screaming, *Why is there a plastic spider on your head?*

"I think we're ready," Matty says. "Cool hair ornament, by the way."

I can't look at Matty. I'm afraid I'll get the uncontrollable giggles. He's always been good at delivering these witty one-liners without cracking himself up. He does it because he knows what it does to me.

"Thanks. Keeps people on their toes," she says, lightly touching the side of her head. "What can I get you?"

"I'll have a buttermilk waffle, a side of bacon, and orange juice."

"I'll have the chocolate-chip Belgian waffle and coffee," I say.

Logan and Spencer both order Farmer's omelets, English muffins, and orange juice, although I notice Logan requests egg whites. Odd. I didn't think anyone under thirty worried about clogged arteries.

It sounds stupid, I know, but I miss Joey. If we were here together, we both would've ordered grilled cheese sandwiches and fries even though it's breakfast time. We loved grilled cheese dunked in ketchup. We also loved the Yankees, zombie movies, the beach (even in the winter), *That '70s Show* reruns, arcades and skee ball, taking the ferry to New York City, and just doing nothing together—sometimes for hours. I miss all those little things. But mostly, I miss the comfort of knowing I can be myself around a guy. He fell in love with me. The real me.

After the waitress brings our drinks, I go to the ladies' room to fix my hair and apply makeup. The guys haven't gotten their food yet, so I'm feeling confident they won't leave without me. This would be the perfect time to call Lilliana, if only I had my phone.

JENNIFER SALVATO DOKTORSKI

How did I get here? I think as I stare into the mirror, carefully lining my top and bottom eyelids. My eyes have looked better, but at the moment, nothing seems right.

I'm feeling only slightly more human when I emerge from the bathroom with smoother hair and copper eye shadow, my summer shade. As I walk down the hallway, away from the restrooms, and back toward our table, I pass a pay phone. Aha! That's it. I need to figure out how to use one of those things. Lilliana gave me a prepaid calling card before I left. She vowed to be my eyes and ears back home. Right now, however, my food is probably out, and I don't feel like getting left behind at a Waffle House in—where am I, anyway?

Matty steps out of the booth and lets me slide in toward the window. "So, when's our next stop?" I ask.

"It's in the—" Spencer says.

"I know, I'll read it when we get back in the car. Can you just answer my question for now?"

"Luray, Virginia," Spencer says.

"What's there?"

"Luray Caverns," Matty offers.

"What's Luray Caverns?"

"Only one of the most famous caves in the entire world." Spencer sounds like I've insulted him.

One of? Are others more famous? Spencer is going on and on about crystallized calcite, stalactites, stalagmites, blah, blah, blah. This dude is all about the caverns. It's kind of cute, the way he's getting so excited. I smile and try to listen (okay, maybe not that hard), but all I can think about is what may be lurking amidst those rocks.

"Uh, are there bats in these caverns?"

"I knew it," Logan says. "You can wait in the car."

"Maybe I will," I say. Great comeback.

I silently obsess about creatures of the night during the rest of breakfast, and after three cups of coffee I totally need to pee before we leave. I drag Matty with me, using the excuse that I need to use my phone in private, but the truth is, I'm beginning to think Logan is serious about leaving me behind.

"Uh, I'm not going in, you know that, don't you?" Matty points from me to the ladies' room door.

"You mean you're not going to line the toilet seat with paper for me? Of course I know you're not going in. Just wait here!"

"Relax," Matty says.

"Sorry. Logan is just such a jerk. He's pissing me off."

"Yeah, that's why you'll be in love with him by the time we hit the Pennsylvania-Virginia border," Matty half mumbles.

"What?"

"You heard me; just pee, will ya."

At least I found out I'm in Pennsylvania.

When we get back to the car, Logan is leaning against the driver's door. He looks at us and makes this lasso/whoop-dee-doo motion with his pointer finger before getting in the Taurus. Is that, like, dork code for hurry up? It's very annoying.

Once we're all in the car, Logan lets out a big sigh before he starts the engine. "Notice how you made two trips to the bathroom and we didn't go at all."

"Yeah, well, I heard holding in your pee causes impotence," I snipe.

This gets Spencer's attention. He stops hooking up his tunes to the car stereo and whips his head around.

"That's not true," Spencer says. "Where did you hear that?"

It's not true. At least, I don't think it is. But Matty the peacemaker jumps in and lightens the collective mood. He picks up the guitar and starts strumming, making up his own words to a Black Eyed Peas song.

"I got a feeling," he sings, "there's a plastic tarantula in my hair. I got a feeling, it's a giant arachnid, but I don't care."

"When did you start playing guitar?" I'm shocked.

"Spence's teaching me. I'd be a lot better if I owned my own guitar," he says.

Huh. How did I not know this? He practically lives on our sofa. I pick up my itinerary as Logan drives back toward the highway.

Luray Caverns, here we come.

Chapter 4

"We're going to Dallas? Why are we going to Dallas?" I sputter.

I'm flipping through the folder Spencer gave me as the Taurus makes its way along Skyline Drive—a 105-mile scenic trip through the Blue Ridge Mountains in Shenandoah National Park, according to Spencer's notes. We've passed lots of rolling, green mountains and two wild turkeys. So far, the scenery is underwhelming and the conversation is lacking. After Luray, we'll head to Nashville, then Memphis, and then, for some strange reason, we veer off Interstate 40 and instead head south to Dallas. Why?!

"Booty call," Spencer says to me. He's tuning his guitar in the front seat.

"What?"

"It's not a booty call," Logan insists. "We're stopping by to see a friend."

I wish they'd both quit saying "booty call."

"You don't just 'stop by' Texas," I say.

"I do," Logan says.

"Must be some friend," Matty says. "What's her name?"

"Avery. We hung out all weekend at a prefreshman orientation a few weeks ago. She'll start ASU in the fall too."

I can see Logan in the rearview mirror. He smiles in a way that really pisses me off.

"And we're going to Dallas because . . . ?" I need more here.

"Avery lives there." I can hear the "duh" in Logan's voice and I don't like it. "We've been talking a lot. She said to visit her if I'm ever in Texas."

"But we're not going to Texas, we're going to Arizona, and it doesn't exactly look like it's on the way."

"It is if my brother thinks he's going to get some. . . ." Spencer trails off.

Logan holds the wheel with his left hand and whops Spencer's head with his right.

"Watch the guitar." Spencer's all jammed up in the passenger seat with the acoustic on his lap. Unfortunately, the case is still hogging up the backseat.

"You should be happy," Logan says in my direction. "You'll have some female companionship for a couple of days."

"Days? Whataya mean 'days'?" I ask incredulously. How well does he know this Avery person?

"We're spending two nights at her house," Logan says.

"All four of us?" Is he serious? Maybe she's the kind of person who invites strangers to her house but doesn't really mean it.

"She says there's plenty of room," Logan adds.

"You should have known all this," Spencer says, turning to look at me. "It's in the—"

I hold up my hand to stop him. "Well, if Logan gets to go to Dallas, then I want to go to Dollywood."

"I thought you hated country music," Matty says.

"I do, but I love roller coasters and Dolly Parton. She's Miley's godmother." I have a secret addiction to *Hannah Montana* reruns.

"We don't have time," Spencer says. "From the caverns we're driving straight through to Nashville."

"So?" I say.

"So, Dollywood is near Knoxville, which is before Nashville. We'd have to spend the night there. That's not part of the plan," Logan says.

"Let's change the plan," I say. "We can stay one night in Dallas, which would give us time to spend one night near Dollywood." And then I say, in a singsong voice for effect, "Probably more girls at Dollywood than at Avery's house."

Spencer turns around again and raises his eyebrows. He looks at Matty, who seems equally intrigued by the idea. Aha, I might have a mutiny on my hands. I give Spencer and Matty a knowing smile and let it drop for now. If I work this right . . . Hooray for Dollywood!

An hour later, we pull into the visitors' center at Luray Caverns. I grab my backpack and follow the boys to the rustic-looking main building, where we each shell out eighteen bucks for the tour and proceed to the cavern's entrance.

There's an eerie chill as we begin our slow descent down the smooth stone walkway inside the caves. Goose bumps rise across my arms. If I weren't so anxious all of a sudden, it would feel like I'm on line for the Pirates of the Caribbean ride at Disney World. I wish I were. Where is Orlando Bloom when you need him?

Darren, our tour guide, is going through his spiel about flowstone and dripstone as we walk along the well-worn pathway. He explains formation after formation—like the Great Stalactite pipe organ, these rocks that look like fried eggs—each illuminated with dramatic lighting. Under different circumstances, I might enjoy the beauty of these ancient sculptures, but it's hard to concentrate because (a) I'm terrified of winged creatures with fangs and (b) I'm wearing a tank top and short shorts and it's freezing in here. A guy toward the front with a kid on his shoulders reads my mind and asks about the temperature.

"The caverns remain at a constant fifty-five degrees," Darren says. Hearing that only makes me colder, not to mention hungry. "Remember, at our lowest point we will be one hundred and sixty-four feet below the earth's surface."

Great. Now it feels like the walls are closing in.

"What time is it?" I whisper to Matty. I'm lost without my phone. I need to get a watch. I need to get air. I need to get out of this cave.

"Eleven thirty."

"How long is this tour?"

"About an hour," Matty says.

"If you'll follow me this way," Darren says. "We're approaching Dream Lake. The lake is only about eighteen to twenty inches deep, but the stillness of the water gives you a perfect reflection of the stalactite ceiling. It's an amazing photo op."

I inhale slowly through my nose and exhale through my mouth. I'm trying to appreciate Dream Lake, but my thoughts wander back to the rock formation that looked like giant potato chips, and that reminds me of the Cheez-Its in my bag. Did Darren say anything about eating on the tour? Screw it. I'm cold, starving, and edgy. I move toward the back of the group, pull out my snack bag as discreetly as possible, and sneak some crunchy squares into my mouth. Everyone else is gawking at Dream Lake and taking pictures, but I hang back, munching away and breathing better with each salty bite.

I'm reaching into my pack for bottled water when it happens: Something makes a dive for my head. I stifle the urge to drop the F-bomb as I drop my bag, spilling Cheez-Its onto the cave floor. My heart is about to explode. I turn in circles and start running my fingers through my hair like I'm giving myself a shampoo. *Please don't be a bat. Please don't be a bat.* My silent freak-out is starting to attract some attention. So much for the captivating beauty of Dream Lake. Matty turns around. A snaky smile spreads across his face as he catches my eye and saunters toward the back of the line.

"Ohmygod, ohmygod, ohmygod," I whisper-scream when Matty arrives at my side. "Matty! Something just dive-bombed me. Is it in my hair? Do you see anything?"

I think Matty will know what to do, but he just stands there, smiling and shaking his head. Joey would have saved me from the bloodsucker by now. That's if Joey would have agreed to explore a cave to begin with, which he wouldn't.

"Matty, is it gone?" I say as I grab hold of his arm and watch the cave ceiling. "Was it a bat?"

"Not a bat," Matty says, "Batman."

Matty bends down and picks up a small plastic figure off the floor. By now, we have attracted the attention of our guide and a few random tourists.

"Is everything okay back there?" Darren asks as he peers around the crowd. Then he spots the Cheez-Its on the ground and his eyes bug out. "Miss, I'd like to remind you that food and drink are not allowed inside the caverns."

It's at this point that I see that man with the kid on his shoulders walking toward me. The kid's face lights up when he sees Matty holding the tiny Caped Crusader.

"You found my Batman," the boy exclaims.

I'm too relieved to be angry. Thankfully, Darren is moving on, and the crowd is following.

"You suck," I tell Matty. I don't even want to look at him as I drop to my knees and scoop up the mess I made. Within seconds, Matty is at my side helping.

"Now, that was funny," he says.

I roll my eyes.

And then Matty starts to sing. "I've got a feeling, there's a plastic Batman in my hair. . . ."

I purse my lips and try not to smile, but I can't help it. The next thing I know, I'm laughing so hard I'm doing sleep apnea snorts and I've got to pee. And you know what? It feels pretty damned good.

Chapter 5

I call my parents as we're pulling away from Luray Caverns. Matty dials for me. He's carrying his responsibility too far. It's so annoying. After what seems like thirty-five-thousand years, he hands me my phone. It's nice to hold my cell again. I miss it. It's like I'm constantly aware of this two-by-three-inch void. After some initial chitchat with Mom about where we are and how I'm feeling, I start to work my magic.

"Guess what?" I say.

"What?" Mom says.

"Logan is taking us all to Dollywood. Can you believe it? I said I wanted to go and he said 'okay.'"

Logan can be a dick if he wants, but now he's a dick on his way to Dollywood.

"You're going to California?"

"No, Ma, Dollywood. In Tennessee."

There's a long pause, and I know it's because Mom is either totally confused by how happy I am to be going to Dollywood or completely dumbfounded by the fact that such a place exists.

"That's great, honey." Mom sounds hesitant. "Have a good time. Let me get Dad. He wants to say hello too."

When Dad finally picks up the kitchen phone, he tells me I need to speak with my lawyer soon.

"His name is Steve Justice."

"Are you kidding me?" I hope this isn't some guy my dad found from a cheesy TV commercial.

"A good friend of mine recommended him. He said Steve knows his way around a restraining order," Dad says. "You're going to have to set up a call with him to answer some questions."

"Okay, will do," I say. "Thanks, Dad."

"Love you," he says, and then he just hangs up. My dad doesn't transition well on the phone. Never has. When the conversation's over, there's no "good-bye" or "talk to you soon." It's nothing but dial tone.

"My dad says admission to Dollywood is on him. I can put it on my emergency credit card." I'm cringing inside at my lie. The karma police are coming for me soon.

What else can I do? If I don't want to spend extra time at some strange girl's house, I need to secure our diversion to Dollywood. Admittedly, I care less about the theme park and more about screwing with Logan's plan. Plus, I don't want them to know I was talking about my lawyer. "Oh, and my mom says to thank Logan for taking such good care of her daughter. Just like you said you would."

Matty raises his eyebrows. He knows when I'm up to something, but I know he wants to go to Dollywood. In my head, I silently promise God I'll pay back my dad.

"Awesome," Spencer says, and pulls out his iPhone. "I'll see if I can get some deets on Dollywood."

Spencer's kid-in-a-candy-store approach to life is very endearing.

My own phone makes the new-text-message noise. I look at Matty. "Am I allowed to read it?"

"Let me see who it's from first."

My stomach does a flippy thing. I don't even want to let myself hope that it's Joey. I'm hurt and mad, but I still want to talk to him. I need closure. It would make me feel so much better if he reached out to me. And then it hits me—can a TRO be violated in reverse?

"Lilliana," Matty says, and hands me the phone. I look at the screen.

YO. GOT INFO. CALL WHEN YA CAN. L8TR. L.

"Can I call her?"

Matty dials and hands me the phone only after Lilliana picks up. What does he think? I'm devious enough to program Joey's number under Lilliana's name? Okay, I am. I just didn't think of it in time.

"What's up?"

"Joey's been talking shit about you," Lilliana says.

"What kind of shit?"

"He's been telling everyone how you put out on your first date."

"What? How do you know this?" I keep my voice even and turn toward the window. I feel Matty, Logan, and Spencer listening. I don't want to give away how upset I am as the state of Virginia passes by in a blur of blacktop and green.

"My brother's working at ShopRite for the summer. He's worked a few shifts with Joey. Says he brags about all the crazy shit he does with the slut. He's been telling every-one you were easy, but she's better."

In our town, at some point everybody either works at ShopRite or knows someone who does. Sometimes, Eddie hangs out with Lilliana's brother. I hope this disgusting lie doesn't get back to him.

I don't say anything for a few seconds. I'm afraid to talk. I don't want to cry. I am trapped in this car with my anger and I can't do anything about it. What a sleazy thing to do, although I guess I can understand Joey bragging about his exploits with my slutty replacement, but why drag me into it? Is this revenge for his car? I'm shocked he wants to hurt me like this.

"You okay?" Lilliana finally asks.

"I'm good. Call you later."

"Sorry. I thought you'd want to know."

"I did. I do. Thanks."

I disconnect and hand my phone back to Matty without looking at him. I'm helpless. As my life in New Jersey falls apart, I'm hundreds of miles away and relying on Lilliana to tell me what's happening. I'm so confused. Is that all Joey wanted all along? To get in my pants? I thought it was enough for him to be *with* me, not *be* with me.

None of this makes sense. Joey had always been completely respectful. Never tried to push me into anything I didn't want to do. He let me initiate things, and mostly, it was just kissing. He seemed fine with that. On Valentine's Day, after we'd been together for about five months, he worked it so we'd have his house to ourselves for a few uninterrupted hours. He ordered out from my favorite Italian restaurant and bought me gold heart earrings. We messed around on the couch for a while. Joey is the best kisser. He has this way of doing things with his mouth that makes a girl want to do more. So, yeah, it was me who said we should go upstairs. I thought I was ready, but once we were actually in his bed together, on the verge of crossing that line, I pulled the plug on the operation. You don't spend two-and-a-half years in an all-girls Catholic school without developing some sense of guilt.

Joey was wonderful about it. He just wrapped his arms around me, turned my chin so he was looking straight into my eyes, and said: "I love you. I'll wait." Then he added, "Your first time should be special. Even if it's not with me. Remember that, Rosie. You are worth it."

At that moment, he felt like a best friend and a boyfriend. I loved having the excitement of "someday" to hold on to and couldn't imagine my first time being with any-body but him. He would wait for me. I didn't realize he meant until someone willing came along. Maybe if I hadn't put the brakes on, we'd still be together. My head hurts. I close my eyes and lean back against the seat.

I don't know how much time passes before I open my eyes again, but when I do, I meet Logan's gaze in the rear-view mirror.

"You aren't getting carsick, are you, Catalano?" Logan asks in his usual, caustic tone. His eyes tell a different story. It's weird, but I can tell he's concerned. Weirder still? The thought of him worrying about me is oddly appealing, making it hard to think of a snarky comeback.

"I'm fine," I say. And leave it at that.

As we're leaving Virginia, we pass a pristine white post fence that seems to go on forever. I try to peer beyond it, look-ing for an enormous farmhouse or mansion in the distance, and that's when I see them, four gorgeous horses on a ridge near the side of the road. One is black with white around its hooves. Two are a coppery brown, and one is a whitish, silvery color—she looks almost iridescent. And I say "she" because, despite her rippling muscles, she has a girly look about her. The horses make me think of Pony, and home. I wonder if my parents are following me on some website, like the airlines do, charting my progress with the GPS.

We pull into a motel in Pigeon Forge, Tennessee, around seven. Dollywood closes in an hour, so we agree to go first thing in the morning when the gates open. It's obvious this unplanned stop is making Logan uptight, but he thinks we can still be on the road to Nashville by sometime tomorrow afternoon and then push on to Memphis the next morning. He's trying to make up time for the Dollywood stop so we can still spend two nights in Dallas. Either he wants to win as much as I do or he really, really likes this girl. Or worse, maybe underneath all the nice talk, he's just like Joey and only after one thing. I hope that's not the case, but if it is, that's more incentive to sabotage Logan's Texas side trip.

The motel room has two double beds. It seems like a waste of money for me to get my own room, and truthfully, I'd be scared. I don't do "alone" very well. I'm relieved when Logan says: "Who wants to find out about getting a roll-out bed?" As much as I hate to admit it, I like the way he handles things. Even though he's bossy, I feel safe with Logan leading this trip.

"Me and Spencer can," Matty says.

"Anyone else starving?" Spencer asks.

"Why don't Logan and I make a food run?" Did I just say that? I can't believe I'm offering to spend time alone in the car with Logan, but I don't feel like sticking around here and trying to wrap my brain around the fact that I'll be spending tonight in a motel room with three guys. Boy, I sure know how to make my parents proud.

It stinks to be back in the car so soon—literally. I didn't notice the boys'-locker-room scent while I was immersed in it. Boys are smelly.

"Let's get Wendy's. I like their salads," Logan suggests.

What's up with this guy? Egg whites. Salads. Hasn't he heard of the Baconator? I want to say, *Get a penis.* But I stick to the topic at hand.

"Fine. But I'm getting a burger and fries. I may need a Frosty, too."

"Emotional eating will get you in trouble."

Now I'm angry that I didn't insult his manhood over the salad.

"Listen, Dr. Phil. I'm hungry. I haven't eaten since that waffle hut, which seems like it was yesterday," I only got, like, two Cheez-Its in my mouth before the Batman attack.

"It's just—you seemed pretty upset after you talked to your friend." We're at a red light and he turns to look at me.

"Glad I could provide some added entertainment. What? Tired of listening to your country music station already?"

"I wasn't trying to listen," he says quietly. "Forget it."

He sounds hurt. Maybe that's why I decide to spill.

"My ex is telling people that I'm, ya know, that we—"

"Didn't you?"

My eyes bug and I whack him on the arm.

"Ow. That hurt, Catalano."

"It works both ways. Whataya mean, 'didn't you?'"

"I'm surprised, that's all. I've seen Joey around school . . . and Matty said you were together awhile."

"So you're surprised I'm not slutty?!" Has that been his impression of me from the start? Is it because he knows the kind of girls Joey dates?

Logan actually looks somewhat embarrassed. His cheeks flush and he backpedals. "No. I mean, there's nothing wrong with it, I just figured—"

Thankfully, we're at Wendy's. "Right. I'm glad you've got me all figured out." I open the car door, slam it hard, and leave him sitting there for a few seconds. Eventually, he catches up with me in the fast-food-line maze. I'm looking up at the menu board as if I don't have it memorized. Logan inserts himself into my line of sight and smiles at me. My stomach goes all spacey. I chalk it up to hunger. He's got a small dimple on the right side. I hadn't noticed. Probably because he hardly smiles.

"I don't have you figured out. I'm sorry. Really."

I avert my eyes from him. I want to stay pissed, but I can't. Especially since he said he was sorry. That's more than Joey ever did. Even when we were together and had our little spats, he was never quick to apologize. "Fine. Buy me a blended chocolate Oreo Frosty and we'll call it even."

"Emotional eating," he says.

I get burger combo meals for me, Matty, and Spencer and then turn Logan over to the Wendy's lady. I smile when I hear him tack my blended Frosty onto his order. He wordlessly hands it to me as we head for the car. I pop the straw in and lean it toward his mouth like I used to do for Joey.

Logan raises one eyebrow as he leans toward me to take a sip, holding my gaze longer than expected. "Aren't you afraid I've got cooties?"

"Cooties don't scare me." But the way my heart speeds up when he looks at me with those honey-colored eyes? That's a different story.

Chapter 6

It's two minutes after nine on Sunday morning and I'm in Pigeon Forge, Tennessee, standing inside the front gate of Dollywood. I should be more excited. I would be if I were here with Lilliana and some girlfriends, or even my family. But my reason for this road trip won't exactly win me a spot on Ms. Parton's next TV commercial. "I just got served with a TRO. I'm going to Dollywood!" I wish I were here under happier circumstances. Wait until my dad sees how much admission for four adults costs. I felt light-headed with guilt when I handed over his Visa.

I unfold my park map, and Spencer and Matty peer over my shoulders. Logan stands apart from us, reading the schedule in front of one of the theaters. I guess he really does love country.

"I say we start with the Thunderhead or Tennessee Tornado," Matty says.

"Or Blazing Fury," I say. "That sounds interesting."

Spencer points to the map's attractions list. "Ooh. What about Star Trek Live? I want to leave time for that. It's a Mad Science presentation. Remember Mad Science camp, Matty?"

I don't question how Star Trek fits into a Dolly Parton theme park. I can't argue with the Dollywood logic; so far this place has something for everyone. It's like the Magic Kingdom of the Appalachians.

"Where're we headed?" Logan asks as he rejoins the group. He's in a surprisingly good mood.

"The Thunderhead," I say.

The dark scruff Logan's got going on makes him look very rock star. For a few seconds, my mind slips into hot-guy fantasy mode, but then Logan makes that annoying lasso motion with his index finger and says: "Let's get moving." I can almost hear my dream bubble pop.

We wind our way through the maze for the Thunderhead. There is this girl with ginormous breasts in a spandex tank top about ten people ahead of us. *Put those away!* I want to scream. I know I'm not one to talk, but I keep my curves tastefully covered. We pass her every time the line moves. If these three morons don't stop gaping, I'm gonna push one of them so hard he'll fall into that cleavage canyon. Finally, we arrive on the platform, where the line splits up and people pair off to wait in cattle chutes for the next coaster to arrive. Spencer and Matty want to ride in the front car. The line for that car is, like, three times as long.

For once, Logan and I agree—we're not waiting. The downside is that I'm now crammed into a tight car with Logan. Our thighs are touching out of necessity, and I try to convince myself that the only reason my heart is yammering away is because I'm anticipating the first big drop. Thankfully, I love roller coasters, so I know I won't go all girly on Logan and grab hold of his arm or anything. The coaster begins its slow ascent, clackety-clacking along the metal tracks. I look off into the distance. The scenery is lush—Tennessee has beautiful rolling green hills. I'm watching some kind of bird with a huge wingspan circle above the treetops when the bottom drops out from under me and we careen straight down, pivoting into a sharp turn at the bottom. Adrenaline rushes through me, and I throw my arms in the air.

"This is awesome!"

"What?" Logan screams.

"This is awe—" But I don't have time to finish before we're falling again.

After a few more fast twists and turns, which press me up against Logan and Logan up against me, the car finally screeches to a halt.

"Looks like Spock and Bones are still waiting for the first car," Logan says. He offers me a hand out of the coaster car. "Bet we have time to ride this one again. You in?"

I try to ignore the tingle when I put my hand in his. "Sure."

After the Thunderhead, we go on the Tennessee Tornado, the Blazing Fury, and the Timber Tower, which looks like a giant circular free fall but falls over like a giant tree, hence the "timber." Spencer shrieks like a thirteen-year-old girl and later explains that he gets vertigo on anything that spins. We end our day at Dollywood with lunch, followed by a show called Dreamland Drive-In, which makes me almost appreciate country music. There's a tell-it-like-it-is raw emotion that I find appealing. It's heartbreak music.

"Three chords and the truth." That's what Logan says when I share my thoughts with him as we leave the show. "Harlan Howard said that."

"Are you sure it wasn't Bono?" I'm being serious.

Logan shakes his head, disappointed. "Let's go. We've got a lot of ground to cover."

Unfortunately, Spencer isn't feeling much better as we leave the park and head for the car. Poor guy, I was hoping food and the air-conditioned theater would help. Spencer is very delicate, I'm learning.

"The only way I'm not going to get carsick is if I drive," Spencer says.

"Knock yourself out, little bro," Logan says. "I'm going to sit in the back and sleep."

"Shotgun!" Matty and I yell in unison like two ten-year-olds. Logan grimaces and takes a quarter out of his pocket.

"Heads or tails." He looks at me.

"Heads."

Logan flips with his right thumb and slaps the coin down on his left forearm. He peeks underneath without revealing the coin.

"Heads."

I wonder if he's being nice and letting me win, or if he doesn't want to be in the backseat with me. Matty scowls. I expect him to demand to see the coin, but he gives in.

"Fine. But if she's sitting up front, we're listening to my

tunes. I put a lot of work into Matty's Playlists for the Road, and we haven't listened to them yet."

Then Logan does his lasso finger motion again. He's not going to be happy when I reach over and bend that finger backward.

"What's on here?" Spencer asks as he hands Matty the cord so he can hook up his iPod to the car stereo.

"The tunes range from epic to apropos of location," he says. "Like this one."

Matty taps the screen and cues up a song. Banjo, upright bass. "Country," I mumble.

"Not just any country," Matty says. "Cash." We roll down the windows. The afternoon sun is still blazing, but Spencer claims he needs fresh air so he won't puke up his veggie kabob. Enough said. I'll put my hair in a twist and deal with the aftermath later. We drive in silence as we head toward the interstate. The air smells flowery and the sky is cloudless. I lean my head out the open window and look at my distorted face in the side-view mirror as I listen to the song about love and burning, fire and desire.

I turn and glare at Matty. "What?" he says, all innocent. "Johnny Cash lived near Memphis."

"We're on our way to Nashville," I say.

"A place he helped to define. He was the youngest living person inducted into the Country Music Hall of Fame," Spencer adds.

"Right . . . so this has nothing to do with me?"

"You flambé one car and now you think every song with fire in it is about you," Logan says. "Get over yourself, Catalano."

"Apropos of location," Matty says. "And epic."

Spencer pokes his head into the backseat and looks back and forth between me and Matty as he speaks. His stomach has settled and Logan is driving again. "Here's what we'll do," Spencer says. He flips to the page in his trip itinerary titled Nashville in One Day. Due to our unscheduled stop at Dollywood, he's modifying the plan to fit what's left of today and part of tomorrow and calling it A Taste of Nashville. "As soon as we arrive, we'll head over to Ryman Auditorium to see if we can get tickets for the Grand Ole Opry tonight because we can't be in Nashville and not go to the Grand Ole Opry. Then we can probably make it over to the Wildhorse Saloon for line dance lessons and dinner before heading back for the show. Tomorrow—"

"Okay, bro. We get it," Logan says. "Breathe."

Spencer shoots him a look. He is undeterred. "Tomorrow, we'll hit the Country Music Hall of Fame and Museum, walk around a bit, have lunch at Jack's Bar-B-Que, and be on the road to Graceland by twelve thirty."

"Sounds like a plan," Matty says.

"Sounds like watching paint dry while someone plays a banjo," I say. Spencer looks hurt, and I wish I could take my snottiness back. Spencer is the last person in the world I'd want to hurt, and I should be thankful we're not spending the evening trying to sneak into nudie bars. A trip with Joey and his friends would have been like a pole dance tour of America. This is a unique bunch I'm traveling with.

Matty gives me a chance to redeem myself. "Jack's Bar-B-Que has ribs. You know you like ribs."

"You're right," I say. "I do love ribs. I'm sorry, Spencer, it was the low blood sugar talking. And the dance lessons sound fun." They don't really, but this is me trying to be more like Matty.

When we arrive in Nashville, we check into a motel before driving over to Ryman Auditorium, where we "luck out" and are able to snag four tickets to the Grand Ole Opry. Whoo. Hoo. Or should I say, yeehaw? From there it's on to the Wildhorse Saloon for country line dancing. I have to admit, Spencer looks pretty good on the dance floor. Matty? Not so much. But watching him try to move his lanky limbs was worth every minute of the hour-long boot-scootin' lessons.

After dinner—I had blazin' wings and a burger—we head to Ryman Auditorium to see a lineup that includes the Charlie Daniels Band ("The Devil Went Down to Georgia" never gets old, apparently), Lee Roy Parnell, Diamond Rio, and some other acts I've never heard of and never, ever want to see again. I know I should be enjoying myself, but I'm homesick. My Jersey Girl soul is shriveling up and dying out here. I'm quiet on the ride back to the motel, and my mood only gets worse when I learn that the pull-out couch is missing a mattress.

"Looks like we're bunking together," Matty says.

"Looks like you're sleeping on the floor, you mean," I snipe. But when I get a good look at the floor, with its faded blue, indoor/outdoor carpeting, I relent.

"Fine," I say. "But if you touch me, I will kill you."

"I was about to say the same thing to you." Matty makes the peace sign and points from his eyes to mine. "I'm watching you."

"Watch away. After I wash my face and brush my teeth, all you're going to see is me sleeping." It's true. I'm exhausted. Both physically and emotionally. I miss Pony curled up on my bed, family dinner at five thirty, day trips to the beach. I want to call Lilliana, but I decide to wait until the morning. I've also got to call my parents for the lawyer's number and then set up a time with his office to discuss my case.

"Matty. Can you text my mom to tell her where we are and that everything is fine?"

"What do I look like?"

"The seven-foot-tall keeper of my phone."

"She's got you there," Spencer says.

"I know, right?" I say. And then I grab a towel and head for the shower. I decide to make it quick. I'll take another one and wash my hair in the morning.

When I come out of the bathroom, Logan and Spencer are sitting at the table by the window and Matty is sitting on the edge of their bed. They're playing cards and half watching a baseball game on TV. I peel away the bedspread and throw it on the floor (I've heard stories about body fluids on those things). Next, I turn up the edges of the fitted sheets and perform my nightly bedbug inspection before I get into the bed on the side closest to the wall. I fold the sheet over the top of the blanket so it won't touch my skin, put an extra pillow in the middle of the bed to keep Matty on his side, then mumble something that sounds like "good night," and before I know it, I'm out.

Chapter 7

When I open my eyes the next morning, Matty is staring down at me, his head propped up on his hand.

"Morning, sunshine," he says. "You fart in your sleep."

"What?!" I'm instantly wide awake. I sit up and smack him with my pillow. "I do not."

"You do," Logan says from the chair by the window. He's reading this thick book with a boring cover. His hair is wet, like he's freshly showered, and he's already dressed. In that instant, he reminds me of my father. "Nothing to be ashamed of. Everybody does it."

I want to die. I don't know if they're telling the truth or teasing me. I kick off the covers, stomp to the bathroom, and open the door. I catch Spencer coming out of the shower mid-stride. He shrieks and it's as if we're on the

Timber Tower all over again, only this time, I scream too and slam the door.

I feel trapped. I'm wearing shorts and a T-shirt without a bra, but I don't care. I bolt for the front door, bed head and all. I plop myself into one of the two plastic white chairs under our motel room window and cross my arms over my boobs. The door opens a few seconds later. Matty sits down beside me and hands me my phone.

"I'm sorry," he says. "You don't fart in your sleep."

I don't feel the need to comment further on my flatulence or lack thereof, so I simply take my phone. "Trust me?"

"Yep." Then he gets up and goes back inside the room.

I look at the clock on my phone. Seven fifty-five. Is there a time difference between New Jersey and Tennessee? Either way, it's too early to call Lilliana. She sleeps until noon if she's not working. This doesn't stop me, though. I'm expecting straight to voice mail, but Lilliana answers.

"Hey," says a groggy voice.

"Hey, you answered."

"I've been leaving my phone ringer on just in case you need me." My eyes fill with tears and I'm too choked up to talk. Lilliana is so not the mother hen type. But it confirms what I've always known. She's a great friend. "Everything okay?"

"Define okay. Does it include sitting outside a motel in Nashville with morning breath, bad hair, and nothing to look forward to but a morning at the Country Music Hall of Fame?"

My voice breaks. I'm crying now and not even trying to hide it.

"Don't be such a wuss," Lilliana says. "There's got to be something else you can do. Maybe you can go shopping and meet up with the guys later. Shopping always makes you happy."

"Maybe," I say. Could I? I've never walked around a strange city by myself, and I'm not sure I want to start today. What I really want to do is go home. Not because of Joey. I just want to feel normal again.

"Can you do me a favor and check the bus schedule from Nashville to New Jersey?"

I mull a possible scenario. As my GPS-enabled phone continues to blip westward in the Taurus with Matty, I can take the bus home and stay with Lilliana.

Lilliana sighs. "Ro. Do you really think that's an option?

What will you do when you get home? Your parents will freak."

"Please, Lilliana. Please just check."

"Hold on."

Can this work? Will Matty tell on me? Sure, he'll be pissed, but if he blows my cover, he'll be risking the wrath of my father. When did I become an evil schemer?

"There's a Greyhound bus leaving at eleven a.m. today that will get you to Newark, New Jersey, at ten thirty tomorrow morning. That's practically twenty-four hours. Do you really want to spend an entire day traveling on a bus, alone?"

Wow. I didn't realize it would take that long. "How much is the ticket?"

"A hundred and thirty-three dollars."

Oh, man. That's a lot of money to put on my emergency credit card, not to mention the Dollywood tickets I charged. My heart races and there's a pulsing sensation in the back of my skull. Can I pull this off? Should I? What will running home solve?

Lilliana interrupts my thoughts. "Rosie, are you still there?"

"Listen, I'll call you in an hour. Can I stay with you if I decide to do this?"

"Of course. I got your back. But even I think staying away until your court date is a good idea. Stop whining and tough it out. You'll feel better about yourself."

I only hear about half of Lilliana's pep talk. I'm plotting. I'll need to stuff some supplies in my backpack for the bus ride since I won't be able to get my bag out of the trunk once the car is locked. I can tell the guys I don't feel like touring the Hall of Fame. Write Matty a note and leave it on the windshield, under the wiper. Then I'll take a cab and get to the bus station before they're done looking at Kenny Rogers's first pair of cowboy boots. With any luck, I'll board the bus before they notice I'm gone. Logan will probably be happy to be rid of me.

"Ro? Are you listening to me?"

"I am. I am. Let me think about this and call you back."

"Don't do anything crazy. You can be very impuls—"

"Yeah, yeah. I know. I'll call ya." I hang up before she can say any more. "Impulsive." That adjective's been attached to my name since I tried to escape the preschool playground when I was four. As the years went on, teachers added "intelligent underachiever" and "determined" to the comments section of my report cards. My mother maintains this is a polite way of saying "stubborn and defiant" but is quick to add that I'm the type of person who is smart enough to do anything she puts her mind to. The problem is, "anything" is rather broad. I'll be the first to admit, I lack focus.

The door opens again, and this time it's Logan. He puts a hand on my shoulder. I'm wound up so tight with thoughts of escape that it's like I melt. His touch feels protective, safe. Can I make the rest of this trip work? Is he a good enough reason to want to?

"We're leaving here in fifteen minutes," he says.

"Fifteen minutes?" So much for giving it a go. "That's barely enough time to shower. How am I supposed to blow-dry my hair?"

"I suggest you bust a move."

Bust a move? Who says that? It's like all Logan's dorkiness is cloaked by that great body. Clark Kent in reverse. I race inside and order the guys out of the room while I shower, change, and toss extra clothes into my backpack. My legs need a shaving, but I have to prioritize. Fourteen minutes later, I step out of the motel room in a brown sundress with my wet hair in a twist, pulling my suitcase on wheels behind me, buoyed by the fact that this may be my last motel checkout with the Geek Squad.

We drive through Starbucks for breakfast and I only get a coffee. Matty asks me if I'm feeling okay. Normally I'd be partaking in a sausage, egg, and cheese sandwich with him and Spencer, but I tell him I'm still digesting my dinner from last night instead of the truth, which is that I'm too nervous to eat. Once again, health-conscious Logan gets some kind of egg-white-wheat-pita-antioxidant something or other. I hold my cup near the air-conditioning vent to cool my coffee as we drive to the Country Music Hall of Fame and Museum. We're supposed to spend an hour or two there before leaving for Memphis.

"I'm going to skip it," I say as the guys get in line to buy tickets. "I'll wait outside."

"Are you sure?" Matty asks. "Want me to stay with you?"

Why does he have to be so nice? It makes me feel extra guilty for what I'm about to do.

"No, no. Go ahead. I'll be fine. I want to get some sun. I'll meet you back here in two hours."

"You shouldn't be all by yourself without a phone." Matty pulls my phone out of his pocket. "Here. Call me if you need me."

"It's okay. You keep it. I don't need it."

Matty raises his eyebrows but doesn't say anything. Can

he tell I'm up to no good? If my plan is going to work, the phone needs to stay with him. I guess I could leave it on the windshield with my note, but what if it got stolen? I guess I have no choice.

"Fine, give it."

He plops it in my open hand like it's a hot potato.

"Just remember, no Joey."

I'm so consumed with escape plans that I wasn't even thinking about Joey. Hearing his name triggers the memory of my dream. *Meet me in Phoenix on the Fourth of July.* Inside, I cringe that my subconscious would even think something like that. Thank God it didn't happen. And anyway, my hair is still wet. I would never reach out to Joey looking like this. It sounds stupid, but I'd need perfect hair and makeup to call him. Feeling good, to me at least, starts with looking good. Sadly, I don't have any other real talents, so I stick with what works.

The guys enter the Hall of Fame, and I'm left standing alone on the sidewalk staring at my phone. I should call my mom. I need to talk to her about my lawyer before I leave my phone behind and get on that bus. Poor Matty. He'll be able to cover his ass for a day or so, but after that, I don't know what'll happen. I'm trying to picture how my going home will play out, but I can't, so I don't. I'm getting on the bus and that's that.

"Hi, honey, how was Dollywood?" Mom asks when she answers.

"Great." It really was. No need to mention things haven't been going so well since. "How's Pony? What's he doing?"

"Sleeping in the corner of the kitchen, big surprise. Pony, guess who I'm talking to? It's Rosie."

I hear a couple of quick woofs. "Aw, don't tease him, Ma. What's he doing now?"

"He's looking out the back door for you." That makes my eyes well up.

"Poor guy. I miss him."

"You'll see him soon enough. Hold on a sec, your dad left me the attorney's number. Should I just text it to you?"

"No, no. I've got a pen right here." I hope I don't sound panicked.

"You're supposed to call his secretary, Miranda, to set up a time to talk."

"Miranda? Steve Justice has a secretary named Miranda. Are you kidding me?"

"What can I tell you? That's her name. Is everything else okay? You sound a little off."

How does she do that? Forget the GPS in my phone, it's like Mom planted a chip in my brain. I try to make an excuse.

"Mom, don't make me point out the obvious here. I'm not in a very good place right now."

"I know, sweetie, but things will get better. You'll see. You know what your *abuelita* always says, don't you?"

I sigh. I hope this isn't going to be a long story. "Abuelita says a lot of things, Mom."

"Lo que no te mata de fortaliece."

"Whatever doesn't kill you will make you stronger? Everybody says that, Mom. Is that supposed to help?"

"It sounds better in Spanish."

"No. It doesn't."

"Te amo, mija."

But that does. "Love you too, Ma. I'll talk to you tomorrow."

I may even see you.

My brain feels fuzzy. I need more caffeine, and I'm suddenly hungry. At the museum's restaurant, I get a large coffee and bagel to go. The cashier tells me the bus station is a five-minute cab ride away, so I've got a little time before I need to head over there. I'd rather hang out here awhile longer. I pick up a free brochure about the Hall of Fame and sit outside on a low wall and read up on this place. Hmm. From the sky, the building was designed to look like a bass clef. The windows resemble piano keys and the edge of the building is supposed to be a 1950s Cadillac fin. I decide to step back to get a better view of the piano keys and fin.

I'm standing about fifty yards away from the building facade, cup of coffee in one hand, bagel in the other, when it hits me. WTF? What am I doing? Am I really going to run away? This tingly sensation comes over me and my heart starts racing. I need to buy something. Anything. I walk back toward the museum. There has to be a gift shop in this freaking place. I look at my phone. Forty minutes until my bus leaves. I wander around the gift shop examining the various guitar-shaped souvenirs, then browse the women's apparel. I pass on the black T-shirt that says GOT COUNTRY? in white lettering, but something about the pink tank that says WELL-BEHAVED COWGIRLS RARELY MAKE HISTORY grabs me. I decide the thirty-five-dollar price tag is worth it. After all, it will be my only souvenir of this adventure. I get the shirt and also buy a Hall of Fame postcard for Matty.

After I leave the gift shop, it's time to put my plan in

action. I call Lilliana and tell her I'll call from a pay phone when I get to Newark tomorrow. She sounds disappointed that I'm not sticking it out but says she'll come and get me. I rummage through my bag for a pen and flip the postcard to the blank side. I write small so everything I need to say fits and end my note with *I'm really, really sorry. Thanks for trying to help me. Love ya, Rosie.* My chest feels tight as I walk to the car. I put the postcard under the windshield wiper on the driver's side and notice I've lucked out. Spencer left his window open a sliver, probably in anticipation of how hot it's going to be when they leave the Hall of Fame. God bless him. I slide my phone through the crack and it lands on the front seat. Excellent. I take a few steps away, then glance back. My breath catches in my throat as I get a last look at the Taurus before turning away to find a cab.

Chapter 8

No disrespect to the country music capital of the world, but I wouldn't want to find myself at the bus station after dark. The terminal is nice enough. Lots of windows. Very blue outside, very white inside. But the neighborhood is a bit sketchy.

As I step through the automatic doors, I immediately get the impression some of the clientele may be too. A man in dirty cargo shorts, worn work boots, and an *American Idol* T-shirt approaches me and holds out his hand.

"Keep hope alive, baby," he says.

I try my best to ignore him and scan the waiting area for an empty seat so I can collect my thoughts for a minute before buying a ticket. A dull ache is forming at the back of my head. I spy an end seat and make a beeline for it. As soon as I plop down, I start rummaging through my bag, pretending to look for something so I don't have to make eye contact with anyone. As I organize the contents of my purse, picking out gum wrapper scraps and old receipts, tattered work boots enter my sight line. I look up to see the man from the door smiling at me with his four good teeth.

"Got a dollar in there, baby? Come on, keep hope alive."

I give him my best northern New Jersey attitude. "How will giving you a dollar keep hope alive?"

He puts a hand to his chest as if he's about to recite the Pledge of Allegiance and says, "Allow me to introduce myself. I'm Hope."

Oh, man. I should have seen that coming. The pain spreads across my forehead. I need Advil. I rub my temples and close my eyes.

"Tell ya what. I'll give you two dollars if you stop following me."

"Deal, baby," Hope says, and I hand him the money, convincing myself as I do that he's going to buy food with it, though his bloodshot eyes tell me a different story. "Have a safe trip, baby, And remember, no matter where you go, there you are."

"Thanks."

I check the time and look over at the maze in front of the Greyhound counter. There's a short line. I take a deep breath. It's time. If I'm going to make that bus home, I've got to buy my ticket now.

I take my place at the end of the line just as a lady at the counter is getting loud with the Greyhound employee. "Try the card again," she says. "I know it's good. I just used it this mornin'."

This is going to take a while. What if I miss my bus? My stomach twists and my heart pounds in my ears. My head may very well explode. Maybe this is a sign that I shouldn't get on that bus. If I leave now, I can get back to the Hall of Fame, retrieve my note, and make up some lie about why my phone is in the car before the boys realize I'm missing. I'm mulling this over as Loud Lady kicks the volume up a notch.

"Maybe it's your machine. Did you ever think of that?"

I peer at the ticket booth as she takes another credit card out of her wallet and slaps it on the counter. "Try that one," she snipes before adding, "jerk." Oh no, she didn't.

Another Greyhound ticket agent steps up behind the counter. He whispers something to his coworker, then opens a second window.

"I can help the next customer," he says.

The line starts moving. He assists two customers while Loud Lady continues her tantrum. Maybe I should try the self-serve ticket kiosk.

"This in UN-believable," she screams. "Someone get me a manager."

And then a horrible thought enters my brain. What if this woman is on my bus and what if she sits next to me? Twenty hours with her instead of the guys—is that what I really want?

If only I had my phone, I could call Lilliana to talk through this. And then I remember the calling card. I scan the room for a pay phone as I simultaneously rummage through my purse to locate my wallet with the card. I spy a phone near the entrance to the ladies' room just as the ticket agent looks at me and says, "I can help you here, young lady."

I step up to the counter.

"Where are you going today?" he says.

Oddly, I hear Hope's voice in my head. *No matter where you go, there you are.* It's the kind of advice one usually finds on a coffee mug, but it's oddly profound.

"Newark, New Jersey?" It comes out like a question. *There I'll be*, I think. *And then what exactly?*

The ticket agent hits some keys on the computer. "That bus will be boarding in five minutes and your total will be one hundred forty dollars and ninety-eight cents with tax. How will you be paying today?"

"Uh, credit card," I say.

I'm about to hand over my emergency credit card when Loud Lady comes unhinged and starts pounding with both fists on the ticket booth glass. I wonder if it's bulletproof. At that moment, a uniformed man who is either a security guard or a real police officer races over and pulls the woman away from the counter. She turns and swipes at the cop's face, but he catches Crazy Ass Lady by the wrist before she can deliver the blow.

"Let go of me," the woman screeches. "You're hurting me." She breaks loose and tries to run toward the door but trips over her suitcase. That's when the law enforcement dude plants a foot on either side of her facedown torso, placing one hand between her shoulder blades to hold her on the floor. With his other hand, he talks to someone using a crackling walkie-talkie-type device. I feel sorry for this strange woman with her face pressed against the dirty bus station floor. Who knows what makes people totally lose it? I could be her.

I close my eyes and replay the scene of Joey walking into that party with his arm around that girl. I was beyond pissed. My first instinct was to get in her face. I know it takes two to tango and all that, but I blamed her for going after my boyfriend. When Joey leaned down and tenderly kissed the top of her head, something inside me broke. I bolted from the party as all my hurt and anger bubbled to the surface. I had to do something.

It was just after one in the morning when I pulled up in front of Joey's house. His Mustang was in the driveway, so I knew he was home from the party. I used his Valentine's Day card to start the fire, the one with the surfing penguin on the front that said FOR ONE COOL GIRLFRIEND. It was so satisfying to click the Scripto lighter and send my valentine up in flames. As it burned, I stared as the ocean wave, the yellow surfboard, the penguin's feet, disappeared. Then I dropped the card on my Joey Box and got back in my car. I had no idea things would go so wrong.

The sound of approaching sirens brings me back to the Nashville bus station. My eyes dart from the screaming woman to the pay phone to the door, where Hope is accosting newcomers. That's when I bolt toward the pay phone.

✳   ✳   ✳

I'm sitting on a bench clutching my bag and sunning my face outside the bus station when the guys pull up to the curb. I couldn't chance a cab getting me back to the Hall of Fame in time. My bus left fifteen minutes ago and I can't imagine being stuck, alone, in Nashville.

Matty jumps out of the rear passenger door. "What the hell is this, Rosie?" he yells as he climbs out. There's something about hearing my name spoken aloud that underscores the big trouble I'm in. I've never seen him so angry. He's waving the postcard in my face. "How could you? What the—you are something, really something."

Yikes. What's six feet tall and red all over? Let him get it all out. I deserve it. After a few more minutes of his huffing and puffing, I say, "Relax. I didn't go through with it. I called you, didn't I?"

"Do you ever think of anyone except yourself? How do you think I would have felt if I read this card and knew you were gone and there was nothing I could do about it? What was I supposed to tell your parents? What if something happened to you between here and New Jersey?"

I shrug. Because I don't have a good answer. He's right. I didn't want to think it through, so I didn't.

He imitates my lame gesture. "That's it? That's all

you've got?" Matty rips my postcard into tiny pieces. He's still yelling, though. "Yeah, well, if you pull a stunt like this again, I'm gonna let you go. Got it?" He throws the handful of postcard confetti in my face. I wince. That I didn't see coming. Tears rise in my eyes.

I shake postcard flakes from the front of my dress. "I'm sorry, okay? What else do you want me to say?"

"You know what? I don't want you to say anything to me for a while. Nothing. Got it? And by 'a while' I mean until we get to Texas. And even then I'm gonna have to think about it." He turns, gets into the backseat, and slams the door.

Spencer gets out of the front seat. "You'd better ride up here, Rosie," he says. "I'll get in the back with Matty." He and Matty are so much alike, always trying to smooth things over.

Spencer is still talking. "The Hall of Fame was great, ya know. Could have stayed there all day. Too bad you missed it."

I've got to get this boy a life or at least a girlfriend, though to him, the latter would probably equal a life. He doesn't have a half-bad body for a skinny kid. Not that I was checking him out when he got out of the shower or anything. But, well, he was right there in front of me. There's got to be a girl somewhere who will go out with him. Now I am staring at Spencer. *Get in the car, Rosie. Look sheepish and repentant.* "You're right. I probably should have stuck to the itinerary."

"At least you didn't miss Graceland," Spencer says. His sincerity makes me want to keep my sarcasm to myself.

I slip into the front seat and Logan nods toward my bag. "Shopping?" His question puts me at ease. One corner of my mouth turns up.

I take my bad cowgirl shirt out and hold it against my torso to model it.

"Nice. Is there a picture of you in handcuffs on the back?" There's something reassuring about Logan being Logan. He doesn't seem mad, even though I must have thrown off the schedule by at least thirty minutes this time. He catches me off guard when he puts a hand on my shoulder. "You know, if it were my decision, I wouldn't have picked you up, right? I would have let you sweat it out."

"Admit it. You would have missed me."

He smiles and I know I'm right.

"You're a real pain in the ass, you know that?" he says.

"I'd like to think it's part of my charm."

Matty snorts from the backseat and launches my phone

into the front, where it lands by my toes. A move that clearly means "Call Joey. See if I care if you screw yourself." Matty and his motherly reverse psychology. Logan, who is either amused or entertained, shakes his head and puts the car in drive while Spencer fires up some old song about going to Graceland.

I lean over to pick up my phone and remember that I'm supposed to call Miranda. First, I send Lilliana a quick text. PLAN ABORTED. EN ROUTE TO MEMPHIS. HUGS, R. Her return text comes quickly. THX FOR THE ANEURYSM. STAY PUT. PROMISE? I type back. SO SORRY, MY FRIEND. CROSS MY HEART. My phone makes the text sound again. But it's not Lilliana, it's Spencer from the backseat. HE'S ONLY PISSED BECAUSE HE CARES . . . A LOT. I type. I KNOW. YOU'RE A GOOD FRIEND. He texts. GLAD U CHANGED UR MIND ABOUT LEAVING. It's hard not to turn around and smile at Spencer. KNOW WHAT? ME TOO. Then I dig out Miranda's number and dial, vowing to make it to Arizona without committing any more misdeeds requiring an apology. Yeah, right.

When Miranda answers, I introduce myself, and she tells me she's been expecting my call. I'll bet. Probably has me down on her calendar as Torch Girl. She asks me to give her a second as she pulls up a fresh Word document, then tells me to start at the beginning and give her a rundown of everything that happened the night of the blowup. Saying it all out loud, again, with an audience (a third of which is very angry at me), makes me feel weird. Out of body. Like I'm talking about some lunatic girl on a TV sitcom. Was this the perspective that my mom was talking about when she tried to convince me this trip was what I needed? I wonder if Mom gets tired of being right.

"Who's she talking to?" Spencer asks Matty.

"Don't know. Don't care," Matty answers. And then he takes out the guitar and starts strumming. I put a finger in my ear so I can block out the background noise and focus on what Miranda is saying.

"Were there any witnesses?" Miranda asks.

"Not that I know of. I went there by myself and I didn't stick around much after I lit the box on fire. But I called Joey from the car and waited until he came outside." I realize how horrible that sounds. I guess it sounds horrible because it is horrible. And hateful, childish, despicable. I decide to keep the part about bringing a Big Gulp along in case the flames got out of control to myself. No need to add "crazy" to the list of adjectives.

"Steve has a guy who does investigations for him. He

might want to send him over there. Every neighborhood has a busybody. Maybe someone saw something that can help with your defense."

She's right. I think about Mrs. Friedman who lives across the street from us.

"Do you think maybe it wasn't my fault? The car part, I mean. I know I can't deny that I torched the box." Things are looking up all of a sudden.

"Don't get too excited. There's still the alleged stalking. You haven't had any other contact with the defendant? That is, aside from driving by his house, seeing him at the mall, and the two text messages you sent."

My body gets hot with embarrassment. The trouble I'm in is serious. This can get bad, real bad. I can hear it now. Guys in my town are gonna be like: Rosie the Stalker? Dude, steer clear of that.

"I don't think so."

"You need to know so. Is there anything else Steve needs to be informed of? We don't want to be in court and hear about any surprise phone or computer records."

Why did I say I don't think so? My last night home and the memory of my Benadryl haze has got me totally unsettled, that's why. But there's no way I'm going to tell

Miranda about that right now, with the guys listening in. Besides, it wasn't real and I don't want to seem more "off" than I already do.

Miranda's voice interrupts my thoughts. "You still there?"

"Still here."

"So, is there anything else?"

"Nope. That's it."

Before we get off the phone, Miranda sets up a time for me to speak with Steve tomorrow. That should work out fine since we'll be in Dallas by then. I'll be able to talk with him privately.

"What's next?" I ask as I end my call.

"Food," Logan says. "Then Memphis."

"Still planning on getting to Dallas tonight?" I ask. I've made a tight schedule a lot tighter.

"Yep," Logan says.

After a quick, and quiet, lunch at a rest stop, we're back in the Taurus and careening down Interstate 40 toward Memphis and the Tennessee border. I'm in the back with Spencer. Matty rides up front. He still doesn't want to be near me. My phone makes its text sound. Spencer: HE'LL COME AROUND. Me: HOPE SO.

I put in my earbuds. My plan is to retreat into my sonic bubble until we get to Graceland. I select a playlist that will cleanse my ears of country music and my memory of the Nashville bus station and my fight with Matty. I've got on my game face, but my stomach is in knots. I can't stand having him this angry with me.

I close my eyes and adjust my sunglasses. As the miles roll by, I occasionally pause my tunes to listen in on the guys' conversation, partly to make sure it's not about me. Paranoid much? Despite the fact that Matty is still ignoring me, he's been unusually chatty since Nashville. All three of them are.

"The UK has given us iconic bands, but the US only produces iconic solo artists," Matty says the first time I pause my iPod. Elvis's abode no doubt sparked this gripping discussion.

I want to say "Metallica," but I turn up the volume instead. I don't want Matty getting all up in my face about music. He's mad enough already. Anyway, it really is hard to throw any American bands into the same sentence with the Beatles, the Stones, and the Who.

An hour later, during another iPod pause, I hear Logan say: "College football is never going to move to a true play-off system."

"They've got to," Matty exclaims. And here I was hoping to be like a wildlife photographer and get an uncensored glimpse into the male psyche to keep me from making another Joey-like mistake. No dice. I hit play and fish around in my bag for that darned trip itinerary. May as well make good use of my time.

The third debate I have the privilege of overhearing is about superheroes. This one surely initiated by Spencer.

"Green Lantern. No question," Matty states.

"Are you kidding me?" Spencer says. "Are you forgetting the Hulk?!"

I wish I could fly off in my invisible plane like Wonder Woman. Upon my fourth attempt at eavesdropping, I finally think I'm overhearing some real guy talk.

"Check out that rack," says Matty.

Without moving my head, I shift my eyes and try to look at the cars on either side of us.

"Where?" Logan asks.

Yeah, where?

"In the right lane. Two cars up."

Huh? How can he tell from back here?

"Pull up next to the car," Matty directs. When Logan does, I see there are two girls, maybe a little older than me, driving together. Their cleavage looks pretty much covered up, so now I'm wondering what Matty's seeing that I don't. Matty rolls down his window and begins gesturing. What is that boy doing?

"The rack," he shouts. "Rack!" I can't believe Matty would talk trash to a girl that way, but then I notice he's pointing to the bike rack on the top of their car. It appears one of their expensive-looking mountain bikes is coming loose.

The girl driving the car, who, upon closer inspection, does have a decent rack, misreads the situation like I did at first. Her windows are closed, but it's not hard to read her "F you." Then both girls give Matty the finger before their car tears off down the highway.

"You tried, my brother," Logan says. "Must be her time of the month."

Nice. That's what guys always assume when they can't understand the complex female mind.

A few miles down the road, Logan swerves sharply to avoid what looks like a piece of crumpled metal in the center lane. Not far ahead, pulled off to the shoulder, are the potty mouth girls. Their rack and one bike have slid onto their trunk, and they're both standing on the side of the road looking at what's left of the other bike, stunned.

"That is *so* satisfying," Matty declares.

Logan beeps the horn as we pass and Spencer rolls down the window and yells: "Enjoy your karma, ladies." I laugh hysterically and wish I could reach into the front seat and high-five Matty, but I'm paying the price for my escape attempt.

"That'll teach 'em to drop the F-bomb on Matty," Spencer says.

"Damn right," Matty says.

When the laughter dies down, the conversation picks back up right where it left off.

"Like I was saying," Spencer says, "if the funding doesn't get pulled, they're going to launch a replacement for the Hubble Telescope in 2018, the James Webb Space Telescope. It's an infrared-optimized space telescope and going to be way better than Hubble."

Oh, jeez. I put my headphones back on and pretend to sleep.

Chapter 9

Logan hands me a camera as soon as we step onto the hallowed grounds of Graceland. "Can you take a picture?"

"Sure," I say. "Matty and Spencer, scooch in."

"No way. This one is all me." Logan holds his hands in the air as if he's envisioning a photo caption and says, "Logan at Graceland."

"Okaaay," I say. "Here we go."

I knew he was all about country, but I had no idea he felt some deep connection to the King. I'm almost inspired. After I snap the picture and Logan approves it, I stop a friendly looking couple and ask them to take a picture of me, Matty, Logan, and Spencer in front of Graceland. Although Matty agrees to be in the photo, I stand between

Logan and Spencer because Matty refuses to be next to me. I look at the photo when the woman returns Logan's camera. Everyone is smiling except Matty, and even though only Spencer's between us, we look miles apart. I can't last until Dallas.

I sidle up to Matty as we're waiting on line for tickets. "Okay, what's it going to take?"

"Did you hear something?" he asks Spencer.

"Define 'something,'" Spencer replies.

"Forget it. I think it was an annoying mosquito," Matty says.

Clearly, this is going to cost me. I try to think about something Matty really wants.

"A guitar," I say. "When we get back and I get my dog-walking business going, I'll save up money and buy you a guitar. I swear. I'll even work at my dad's factory if I have to. Any kind you want, name it. But please, can you forgive me, Matty? I can't not talk to you until Dallas."

"Wow. Any kind?" Spencer says. "She has no idea how much a good guitar costs, does she?"

"In case you haven't noticed, she has no idea about a lot of things," Matty snaps. "But begging. That's a step in the right direction."

My cheeks burn with anger. I clench my fists to keep from smacking him in the back of the head. I guess this is Matty's way of saying this is going to cost me more than I thought, maybe even more than a guitar. I'm going to be walking lots of dogs. I relax my hands. It's okay. I deserve it. Plus, if it buys Matty's forgiveness and ends the silent treatment, it will be worth it. I'm about to tell him to name his price when he makes an unexpected reversal.

"You don't have to buy me a guitar, Rosie." It's the first time he's looked me in the eye since showering me with postcard confetti at the Nashville bus station. "How about this? No more escaping and try to have a good time, or at least pretend you're having fun."

I think I'd rather buy him a guitar. "Okay. But it's not like you guys are making it easy for me to have fun. Logan's got his rules and seems perpetually pissed at me. Spencer has his itinerary. You, well, you tease me."

"I always tease you."

"But now I'm outnumbered."

"She is easy prey," Spencer offers.

Matty considers this. "Okay, I can't speak for them, but I'll try if you try."

"Deal." I throw my arms around his skinny middle. "I'm sorry," I say into his T-shirt. He pats my back tentatively.

"You always are, Rosie."

The famed home of Elvis is set back from the main road, behind wrought iron fencing. Graceland is nice, but to be honest, I was expecting a Tara-like, southern mansion. I guess it's the biggest house in the neighborhood, but I've seen better on *House Hunters International*. The fourteen-acre property may be more beautiful than Graceland itself.

We take the audio tour of the house that includes Elvis's living room, music room, dining room, kitchen, TV room, pool room, and infamous Jungle Room. It's like a trip through the seventies. I try to picture normal, family stuff going on here, but it's hard. I mean, just being Elvis is as far from normal as a person can get.

Once outside the house, we visit the family grave site, which is situated beside a circular fountain, and then walk down the long drive to the street. People have written their names and Elvis-centric phrases in chalk and marker on the brick columns of the gate. Logan is at the ready with his Sharpie. The boys pass it between them while I look up and down Elvis Presley Boulevard. Finally, Matty taps me on the shoulder and hands me the black permanent marker. I find space near the gate entrance and write the title of an Elvis tune I know from the Greatest Hits album my parents own: "Hard Headed Woman." Matty peers over my shoulder. "Progress," he says.

At a nearby souvenir shop that sells knockoff, discount Graceland merchandise, I buy an Elvis mug. He's sporting a flamingo-colored jacket with black lapels and standing in front of Graceland beside a pink Cadillac. GRACELAND, HOME OF ELVIS, it says. I get a different Elvis mug for my mom, an Elvis clock that swings its hips for my dad, and an Elvis watch for Eddie that I intend to "borrow" until I get home. I also buy a disposable camera. My parents offered to let me bring their digital, but at the time I was too steeped in bitterness to even envision wanting memories of this journey. At the register, I spot a guitar key chain. I get it for Matty. I slip it into his pocket after we leave the shop.

"Until I get you the real one."

Matty puts a hand on my shoulder and looks me right in the eye. "Ro, forget it, really. It's okay," he says softly.

Even though he lets me off the hook, I know I don't deserve it. Matty, however, deserves a guitar. My family took at least two vacations every year for as long as I can remember, but Matty, he hardly went anywhere. His mom is always working, and they can't afford expensive trips. This is Matty's first official getaway and so far all I've done is, well, be me. And that's hardly good enough for someone like Matty.

For the first time since being served with a TRO— maybe even since Joey cheated on me—I feel like the fog that's been hovering over my brain is finally lifting a little. I think I'm having some kind of spiritual awakening here at Graceland, and I'm not even a fan of Elvis's music. By the time we walk back to the Taurus, I'm determined to make a fresh start on this trip. If only my hair looked better, I think as I catch my reflection in the car door window before getting into the backseat.

Logan merges onto the interstate heading west and we drive across the high-arch bridge that spans the mighty Mississippi River and connects Memphis to Arkansas. The lights dancing on the water look so pretty. Part of me wishes we weren't leaving. It's been a looong day of driving. Originally, we were supposed to stay the night near Graceland, but Logan is determined to get us back on schedule. His schedule, which I messed up. So I guess I have only myself to blame for how tired I am and the way I look right now. I have only me to blame for a lot of things, and that really sucks. Was I really in Nashville this morning? It seems like days since I slipped two bucks into Hope's hand.

I try to fix my hair at a road stop in Arkansas. I'm going to be meeting Logan's girlfriend in a few hours, and I don't want to look like complete and total crap. But it's no use. My locks have suffered a double whammy. I didn't blow-dry my hair with my round brush and I pulled it back in a twist while it was still wet. I give up on my hair and focus on freshening up my makeup. As I exit the bathroom, I stop at the vending machine and get a diet soda. I try to remember what the guys have been drinking. I know Matty likes Gatorade, so I buy him a lemon-lime and settle on two bottled waters for the brothers. I'm sure they won't object. I also buy four bags of chips—baked for the brothers, salt and vinegar for me and Matty.

Logan and Spencer seem surprised when I get to the car and hand them their chips and waters. Matty just says "thanks." He's been around my house long enough to know that it doesn't matter if we're home or away, we like to feed people. It's the Catalano way.

"You look tired," I tell Logan.

"Kinda." He rubs the stubble along his chin.

"Want me to drive? I don't mind. If you'll turn over command of the Taurus, that is."

JENNIFER SALVATO DOKTORSKI

He hesitates for a moment and then gives me the keys, prompting Spencer and Matty to yell, "Shotgun."

"Forget it," Logan says. Deflated, they retreat to the backseat.

The sun is setting as I drive along Interstate 30. As we near the Arkansas-Texas border, we pass the town of Hope, which immediately calls to mind my bus station buddy. It's the birthplace of former president Bill Clinton—they've even got a highway sign that says so. And not far beyond that sign, I notice some unusual roadkill on the shoulder. I squint, trying to make out what it is.

"Armadillo," Logan says.

"No way."

"Never saw an armadillo before?"

"I'm just a girl from New Jersey," I say without a hint of sarcasm.

"You're living now, Catalano," he says. "See what you would've missed if you got on that bus?"

Spencer and Matty play guitar in the backseat for a while. Spencer is helping Matty learn the chords to "Master of Puppets"—great metal never dies. Eventually, though, they both fall asleep and Logan turns on the radio. I'm surprised when he bypasses the country station and settles on something more alt rock. Now we're talkin'. I'm even more surprised that he knows and likes the song enough to play air drums.

"Can I ask you something?"

"You just did."

I've rolled my eyes so many times on this trip, they're going to get stuck that way. "Why ASU? What made you want to go so far away from home?"

"Wanderlust."

I don't say anything. I'm trying to imagine what it would feel like to want to leave my family to go to college thousands of miles away. I like where I live. All my fantasies about the future involve me, a husband, and my hometown. College has always been this hazy notion in the periphery. Logan must mistake my silence for stupidity.

"'Wanderlust' means—"

"I know what it means. Jeez. I'm not an idiot."

He just raises his eyebrows in a don't-make-me-answer-that face. I push on with my interrogation.

"But Arizona?"

"I visited Tempe and could picture myself living there. The desert was like nothing I'd ever seen before. Plus, ASU has a great sustainability program."

He holds up the book he's been carrying around. I glance at it. *"Sustainability: A Global Approach to . . ."* a big long phrase I don't feel like reading.

"Uh, yeah. Now you've lost me."

"It has to do with the sustainability of environmental resources and how that relates to economics, sociology, politics—"

I hold up my hand and cut him off. "Enough. It's now become clear to me that you, too, are a total nerd."

"I'll take that as a compliment." Logan gives me a half grin and the dimple makes another appearance. My heart does a grand jeté.

"Can I ask you another question?"

"Shoot."

"Why air drums?"

Logan chuckles. In fact, I almost make him full-out laugh. I can tell.

"Probably the same reason you randomly belt out one or two words from whatever song you're listening to on your iPod."

I'm glad it's dark so Logan can't see how red I am. "I don't do that, do I?"

Logan turns toward me and rests his hand on my

thigh, which makes it hard to concentrate on the road.

"Yes. Yes, you do."

I scrunch my eyebrows and consider this. I guess I get caught up in my tunes sometimes. "Now I feel stupid." What else is new?

"No worries," he says, then mumbles something that sounds suspiciously like "It's cute."

"What was that?"

"I said it makes me want to puke." He's looking out his window now. I have this urge to touch his thigh. Despite his cranky personality, urges are piling up where Logan is concerned. I'm not happy about that, but it's the truth. So, I keep my hands at ten and two and stare straight ahead at the stretch of highway illuminated by the headlights.

Logan changes the station again. My reprieve from country music is over, apparently. The song is pretty, though. It gives me chills and makes me want to slow dance with a cowboy.

"Who is this?"

"Who is this?" Logan is incredulous. "It's only George Strait. He is country music. Do you know any country singers at all?"

"Keith Urban."

"Because he's hot?"

"Nooo. Because he's a kick-ass guitarist. And he's in *People* magazine a lot."

"I knew it."

"I make no apologies. I like celebrity gossip magazines and hot guys."

"What about college?" Logan asks.

"That was a non sequitur."

"Where are you thinking of applying?"

"You mean *if* I apply. Somewhere in New Jersey. I'll probably wind up commuting."

"How are your grades?"

"B-ish." I pause. "Occasionally more C-ish than B-ish."

"Test scores?"

"You sound like my dad. I'm not telling you my SAT scores!" I say this louder than I intend to and wake up Matty.

"What about SATs?" Matty pipes in from the back. What can I say about a guy who wakes up at the sound of "SAT scores"?

"Logan asked me my scores."

"Logan. You should know better than to ask a lady her SAT scores."

"I didn't ask a lady, I asked Rosie," Logan fires back.

"Ha, ha. How original," I say. "Did you pull that one out of your third-grade joke collection? What's next? A pickle joke?"

"Tell him your scores, Rosie," Matty says. He's chuckling, and we both know why. I kicked butt. Well, not in the traditional Ivy-league-bound kind of way, but in the "Oh, this is Rosie and we're surprised she even took the SATs" kind of way. Low expectations give me the gift of surprise sometimes.

I change the subject. "So, Avery is okay with us getting in tonight? It's pretty late."

"She said it's fine. We'll be staying in the pool house, so it's not like we'll be disturbing anyone."

"Pool house? Who has a pool house?" Country club snobs, that's who, I want to say.

"Your parents?" Matty offers.

"Yeah, it's called 'where I live'! And it's an aboveground pool." This time, my booming voice wakes Spencer. In the rearview mirror, I catch him running his fingers through his hair as he squints out the window. The messy look works for him. I should mention it.

"Where are we?" Spencer says through a yawn.

"Almost to the Texas border," Logan says.

Texas. This will be my sixth state in three days. Seven if you count the drive through West Virginia. I didn't actually set foot in that state so I'm not sure.

We ride on into Texas without speaking until it's time to exit the highway. Then Logan gives me step-by-excruciating-step directions to our destination. Two illegal U-turns later, we arrive.

"Holy shit!" Matty shouts when we finally pull into the driveway of Avery's house, or perhaps the correct word would be "compound."

The half-mile driveway ends in a circle with a fountain in the middle. Graceland has nothing on Avery's digs. The house looks like it belongs in the French countryside, not outside Dallas. I don't know what I was expecting after Logan mentioned a pool house. I guess I was envisioning a big ranch, not a palatial French manor.

"I wonder where the heliport is," Spencer whispers.

"You read my mind," I say as I stare at the imposing mansion. Yet again, I'm totally out of my league.

Chapter 10

I put the car in park, not sure if it's okay for us to leave it here beside the fountain. Then one of the blue double doors opens, and a petite blond girl with glasses peeks her head out. She gives us the one-minute hand signal and then re-emerges in shorts, a T-shirt, and flip-flops. Adorable. Logan steps out of the car and they give each other a friendly but not too, too friendly hug. Still, I realize I'm holding my breath and frowning a little. Logan holds the passenger door open for Avery, then climbs into the back with Matty and Spencer.

"Hey, y'all. I'm Avery," she says, and she turns around and points. "Let me guess, Spencer, Matty."

"Right!" they say in unison like double dorks.

"Rosie," I say.

"Nice to meet you, Rosie. You too, boys." Her smile is genuine, and I think I may like her even though I'm not sure why or if I even want to. "Why don't I show you where to park while you're here?"

We pull around the side of Buckingham Palace, and Avery points to a spot alongside the five-car garage.

"This is good," Avery says. "Grab your things. You can meet my dad and then I'll show you where you'll be staying."

We walk into a kitchen that looks like it belongs on a cable home design show. Tile floors, granite countertops, cherrywood cabinets, and—holy crap, look at that restaurant-size stainless steel refrigerator.

"Daddy? Logan and his friends are here."

An attractive man with salt-and-pepper hair emerges from the family room off the kitchen. He's barefoot and wearing chino shorts with a pull-over green polo.

"Welcome," he says, and shakes all of our hands. "Help yourselves to whatever you need while you're here. My wife is working late, but you'll probably meet her tomorrow."

"Come on, Rosie," Avery says. "I'll take you upstairs to your room and then I'll show the boys to the pool house."

"Why don't I get them set up out there, sweetheart?" Avery's dad offers.

I know I didn't want to come here, but these people are so stinkin' nice, I can't help but like them. Avery and her dad are so warm and down-to-earth. My reservations about feeling uncomfortable melt away.

Avery leads me up this winding staircase in the main entrance hall.

"We have a guest room," she says, looking back over her shoulder, "but I thought it might be fun for you to bunk with me."

Why? I wouldn't think it would be fun to have a sleepover with a complete stranger, especially if that girl is under a TRO and has an impending court date, but what do I know. Maybe this is the way they do things in Texas.

Avery's room is gorgeous—and huge. She has her own bathroom with a vanity and sunken tub, a walk-in closet that's almost as big as my bedroom at home, and a giant flat-screen TV on the wall in front of her bed. "The couch pulls out," she says. "My room is sleepover friendly. It's how my mom compensates for never being around. She lets me have friends stay whenever I want."

"She works a lot?"

"Only all the time. Take my bed. You're the guest."

"No, no. That's okay. I can't take your bed," I say.

"You sure?" she asks. "I want you to be comfortable."

"Believe me, after the motel beds I've been sleeping in, I'll be comfortable. Thank you for letting us all stay here. It's really nice of you," I say. "Are you sure two nights is okay?"

"It's no trouble at all," she says. "It'll be fun."

We stare at each other in silence for a few seconds, not in a bad way or anything, before I begin fumbling with my suitcase. I'm not sure what to say, but Avery is all over the elephant (i.e., me) in the room.

"So," Avery begins. "I know we just met and all, but when Logan called me, he mentioned that you'd gotten into a minor mess and that your parents were making you come along."

"Minor? Did he say I blew up my ex-boyfriend's car?"

Avery is trying to suppress a smile. She's struggling so hard to be polite to this psycho in her bedroom that it makes me laugh.

"I'm not carrying matches or a lighter. Swear. But if you want to change your mind and put me in the guest room, I completely understand."

Avery starts laughing too. "Did he deserve it?"

"He was cheating on me."

"Poop head."

"I know!" I'm so grateful she's on my side, I forgive the fact that she said "poop head." She is just too cute in a non-slutty Barbie kind of way.

"You should have blown up her car too."

I smile. It's funny how a person can go from being a stranger to a friend with just one sentence. "She's not old enough to drive."

Her eyes widen. "Get out. Skank."

"Total skank."

"My boyfriend and I were together for four years when he cheated on me."

"Four years!" I shout, louder than I intended. But I can't imagine what I would have done to Joey if he'd screwed around on me after we'd been together that long. It would have cost him a testicle, I think.

"I wasted my high school years on him. I'm determined not to let it happen again in college," Avery says.

Hmm. Maybe Logan is barking up the wrong tree, then.

"Got a picture?" Avery asks.

"Huh?"

"A picture of the ex? Got one?"

I remember I'm still in possession of both my phone and a few lingering Joey photos that I haven't been able to delete, not yet. I pull up a close-up of him. I remember when I took this. It was October, my favorite time of year next to summer, and we were on our way to the homecoming game. My stomach wrenches when I look at it. I wonder when and if I'm ever going to have these kinds of memories of a guy again. Will taking pictures feel like I'm trying to capture the good stuff before it all goes bad? Right now, it's hard to imagine the exciting part of falling in love. The hurt of the crash landing is still too fresh. I hold up my phone for Avery.

"Hello, blue eyes. I don't blame you for losing it," Avery says.

I can't speak, but the tension goes out of my shoulders. It's nice to have someone understand.

"Feel like going for a swim?" Avery asks.

"Sure."

"Come on, then. The pool is awesome at night. You can kick back in the hot tub, too. Traveling with three guys must be getting old."

"Totally!" I say. Finally. After three days and fifteen hundred miles of nonstop testosterone, a sympathetic face.

The night air is balmy, but the water feels even warmer as I sit on the side of the pool and dangle my feet in the deep end.

The boys emerge from the pool house all suited up. Logan has abs and pecs to match his biceps and a sexy trail of hair that begins just above his belly button. But who's looking? Joey had boyish good looks, but Logan is more man, inside and out. I'm relieved when he jumps in the pool and I can wipe the drool off my chin without anyone noticing.

Avery takes off her terry-cloth poolside dress to reveal an adorable halter-style bikini. She has a lean, muscular runner's body. If she's a cheerleader, she's definitely the one who gets put on top of the pyramid. She steps onto the diving board and dives in. Spencer and Matty cannonball after her, but I suddenly feel self-conscious about my ample boobage and don't want to take off my T-shirt just yet. I've been on the road with these guys since Saturday and I thought I was starting to feel like one of them. But right now, the idea of being half naked around them would be too weird. It's stupid, I know. Matty has seen me in my bathing suit hundreds of times. When he's not living in our house, he's living in our aboveground pool.

Matty pops his head up near my toes.

"Why aren't you coming in? You love night swimming."

"Don't rush me."

Matty lightly splashes my legs. He knows I hate that. I

retaliate by smacking the water's surface with the bottom of my feet. I anticipate his next move and snatch my legs out of the pool before he can pull me in. But I'm too late. Hands grab my shoulders from behind and push me into the deep end. At least now I have an excuse for keeping my shirt on. I let myself slip underwater and pull the twist out of my hair before I break the surface. It feels good, like I'm cleansing myself of road grime—cheap motel soap, the car's lingering french fry smell, random germs from rest stop bathrooms. I'm so relaxed I forget about being pushed in.

"I can't believe you're not even pissed at Logan," Spencer says.

"It was Logan?" I'm still not angry but play along anyway. "You know what they say about payback. And I've got a strong track record."

Avery starts laughing. "Sleep with one eye open, Logan. One eye open."

This pool is amazing. Its low end has built-in seating, like an underwater shelf, and the heat rising from the hot tub makes me think of witches' brew. I love the lulling sounds of summer bugs chirping and the hum of the pool filter. I float toward the deep end as I watch Logan and Avery in the shallow. He grabs her around the waist and throws her a good three feet into the air. She swims underwater and body checks his feet out from under him. I'm grabbing hold of the side, trying to suppress my jealousy and determine what, if anything, is going on between them when Matty swims up beside me.

"Race ya," he says. "To the low end and back." And just like that, we're kids again.

"One, two—" I don't wait, I push off. But so does Matty; he knows I never wait for three.

I slice through the water as fast as I can, doing my best freestyle. I make a swimmer's turn and kick off from the side of the pool, but despite giving it my all (I'm quite competitive when I want to be), I lose to Matty by a whole body length.

"You beat me bad that time."

"That shirt is weighing you down. Take it off for the second heat."

"Nah, that's okay. I'm ready to get out anyway."

I swim over to the ladder and step out.

"There're towels by the pool house," Avery calls. "Help yourself."

I find a stack of plush, sheet-size towels on a rack outside the pool house door. It's like being at a hotel. I peer in the French doors and am completely blown away by the boys' digs. There's a pool table, several old-school arcade games like Ms. Pac-Man and Donkey Kong, and two sets of sectional leather sofas, which I'm guessing pull out into beds. Even if they don't, they look plenty comfy as is. Holy shit. What does Avery's dad do for a living?

I wrap myself in a plush, blue towel and sit on a stool at the resortlike wet bar, where I left my phone before I got in the pool. I do a quick check for messages. Nothing. I fire off a text to my mom. MADE IT TO TEXAS. ALL GOOD. XOXO. LUV U. It's late, but I know she won't sleep until she hears from me.

A few minutes later, Matty, Logan, and Spencer grab towels and join me. Avery scoots behind the bar and opens the mini-fridge. Matty sits on the stool beside me and puts out a hand. Without exchanging a word, I give him my phone for the night. It's just as well. After showing Joey's picture to Avery, I'm feeling vulnerable.

"This thing is stocked, ya know," Avery says. "We've got beer, fruity drinks, wine, soda, water. Who wants a beer?"

"I'll just have a water," I say. Honestly, I don't like the taste of alcohol that much.

"Guys? Beer?"

I can sense Matty hesitating to see what the guys will do. I don't know why, but I'm surprised when Logan says: "I don't drink."

"Not ever?" Avery says. Guess she's surprised too.

"Hardly ever," he says. "Growing up—"

Avery, who is looking at Logan, seems to recall something. She holds up her hand. "Say no more. I remember."

I'm confused. I look back and forth between Logan and Avery as some shared piece of knowledge passes between them. I don't like not knowing what they're talking about. It stings to be left out.

Spencer brings me out of the dark. "I guess you told her we're the spawn of a mean drunk?" He says it matter-of-factly, like it's no big secret, which makes me feel even worse.

Logan answers Spencer with a shrug that confirms he did and remains quiet, but Spencer keeps talking. "Yeah, our dad doesn't know when to say when."

Why didn't Logan tell me? He could have mentioned this during our heart-to-heart in Arkansas. Even though it's not her fault, I don't like Avery knowing something I don't. These are my guys.

A few awkward moments pass before Avery speaks. "Well, I'm the spawn of a renowned cardiologist." She grabs a bottle of white wine and begins to open it with a corkscrew. "And she approves of drinking one glass of wine a day."

"Isn't red wine the one with all the antioxidants?" Spencer asks. No one acknowledges him.

"Does she approve of *you* drinking one glass of wine a day?" Matty asks.

"I don't know. She's not home enough to tell me what she thinks." She doesn't hide her bitterness. "And as long as no one is driving, my dad won't say anything. He knows after I leave for college next month, I can drink whenever I want."

My brain is still running in circles about Logan and Spencer's father. How mean is mean? I wonder. Did that play into Logan's decision to go to college two thousand miles from home? Wanderlust, bullshit. Surely Arizona State isn't the only college in the country to offer a sustainability major. I watch Avery pour herself a glass of wine.

"Can I have one too?" I ask, suddenly wanting to appear more like Avery.

"Of course," says Avery. She hands me the glass and pours herself another. "Matty?"

"I think I'll stick with a beer," Matty says. I promptly shoot him a look. When Avery bends down to look in the mini-fridge, I mouth: "Only one." Matty may think he's in charge of me during this road trip, but I'm still older. Matty never drinks, and I don't want him getting carried away. But at the same time, I don't want to embarrass him in front of a cute girl.

"So, your mom's a cardiologist?" Matty asks. "Do you want to become a doctor too?"

Polite conversation or flirting? It's hard to tell with Matty.

"Me? No. I want to help people in some way, though. My dad is a social worker. I thought about that for a while, but I'm more interested in the big picture. That's what drew me to the sustainability major at ASU. I've also been looking into the Peace Corps for after college. This summer, I'm going to work for Habitat for Humanity."

The Peace Corps? Habitat for Humanity? "Wow," I say. No wonder Logan likes her. They've got a lot in common. I'm slightly envious that Avery knows what she wants to do with her life. I'm slightly envious of Avery, period. I'm starting to feel silly that I never once considered leaving New Jersey, especially not for some underdeveloped country. Painful shots, giant insects—not my thing. But what have I done for mankind lately beyond contributing a gift to the Toys for Tots booth at the mall every Christmas?

"What about you?" Avery asks me. I've been quiet, and I can tell she's being nice and trying to bring me into the conversation. "Any ideas about what you wanna be when you grow up?"

Uh, Joey's wife. That would have been my answer a few weeks ago. What do I say here? To be honest, I've thought about applying to the Fashion Institute of Technology in the city. But I haven't told a soul, and I don't want anyone laughing at my dream of designing wedding gowns right now. "I'm not sure," I say.

I sound stupid and immature, and not at all like the kind of girl whom Logan would confide in or drive hundreds of miles out of his way to visit. I'm recognizing how much I want Logan to see me as more than just this impulsive, pain-in-the-ass, emotional overeater. I'm not giving him much to work with, am I? I'd pick Avery too. Suddenly, I feel drained. If I close my eyes, I think I might fall asleep on this bar stool. I push my unfinished wine away. Avery finishes her drink and turns to me. "You 'bout ready for bed? Y'all must be tired."

"Exhausted," I reply.

"Not so much," Matty says.

"Mind if we check out those video games?" Spencer asks.

"Make yourself at home. The pool house is all yours. Me and Rosie will see you at breakfast. Anyone want to go for a morning run?"

She puts her hand on Logan's shoulder as if she already knows his answer.

"Sure," Logan says. Spencer nods.

"Maybe," Matty says. Maybe? That boy doesn't run unless the basketball coach makes him do wind sprints. Is Matty trying to make a move on a girl Logan's into, a girl who also happens to be two years older than him?

"Okay, I'll come by for y'all around seven."

Seven? Ha! That seals the deal. Matty will still be drooling on his pillow.

"What about you, Rosie?"

I'd get winded before I made it to the end of the driveway. "Uh, I don't even own running shoes. But breakfast, I'm there."

"We can get mani-pedis afterward."

"Now you're speaking my language," I say. I give the boys a half wave and feel a pang of separation anxiety. Why? I'm not exactly sure. I should be thrilled to get away from them for a night. I shake it off and follow Avery into the house and up to her room, where, after a shower in her private bathroom, I collapse on the pull-out bed. I'm in that weird state between dreamland and consciousness when Avery's voice pipes up in the darkness.

"We hooked up, ya know."

"Waa?" I mumble. I meant "who," but it didn't come out that way.

"Logan and I. We hooked up."

"Tonight?"

"Back in May. At prefreshman orientation. I let things go a bit too far. I feel kinda bad about it."

Her words blow through my brain like a cold front clearing away heavy humidity. How far is too far? *None of your damned business, Rosie,* says the part of me that wants to be a polite houseguest.

"Anyway, I thought you should know. I see the way he looks at you. Don't get me wrong, I like having Logan as a friend. We're into the same things, he's fun to talk to and text and all that, but like I said, I don't want to start college as someone's girlfriend."

"I don't blame you," I say.

"For hooking up with Logan or wanting to stay single?"

"Both." I appreciate her honesty and want to return the favor.

We're silent for a couple of seconds before I ask, "How does Logan look at me?"

"The same way you look at him, silly," she says. I can hear the smile in her voice. "Night, Rosie."

"Night, Avery." I hope she hears me smiling back.

Chapter 11

"Joey called."

I open my eyes slowly. I'm not sure where I am and if I'm hearing properly. A girl's knees come into focus. Avery. Now I remember. I rode into Texas yesterday in a Ford Taurus with Matty, Logan, Spencer, and one guitar.

"What?" I sit up, trying to shake the sleep off.

"Matty told me. Joey called. Mister Blue Eyes. That's him, right?"

My heads swims with a mixture of curiosity and anxiety. "Yes. When? What did he say? Did Matty talk to him? Did Joey leave a voice mail?"

"I don't know the specifics. After our run, Matty was going to tell you himself, but I wasn't sure how you'd feel about him barging in here first thing in the morning. I told him I'd give you the message."

"Thanks, but I'm okay with Matty barging in. That's normal at my house."

I throw off the covers and get out of bed.

"Y'all are pretty close, huh?"

I don't feel like talking about Matty right now. I feel like running downstairs and finding out what the deal is, but I pause for a second and try to be polite. "Close? I guess. Like siblings that don't always get along."

"But you're not siblings. And you don't always fight," Avery says with a knowing smile that I choose to ignore. Is she stalling? Is this about Matty or is this about her not wanting me to find out what the hell Joey said? I'm getting agitated. Who am I kidding? I am agitated. Lately, I'm always agitated.

"Uh, where's Matty?"

"In the kitchen with the boys helping my dad cook breakfast."

"Cool." I'm about to go downstairs, bed head and all, when Avery steps between me and the door. My chest tightens and I'm finding it difficult to take deep breaths.

"Ah, ah, ah," she says. "Hold on. You don't want those

three to think you're dying to talk to Joey, do you?"

"But I am. Matty knows that."

I'm resisting the urge to fling her ninety-pound body out of my way and run to the kitchen to find out what Joey said—and call him back. *Breathe, Rosie, breathe.*

"This is the guy that cheated on you and called the police, remember? Before you do anything crazy, think about why he's calling you. Does he want to get you in more trouble?"

Why does she care? Would I care what Avery did if the situation were reversed? I look at her face all cute and serious, and still a bit sweaty from that run, I might add. Now I feel guilty, especially for wanting to fling her tiny body across the room.

"Maybe I'll shower first. My hair's a mess."

"Good girl. You can shower in here."

"And shave my legs. That's what I'll do."

"Now you're talkin'. I'll use my parents' bathroom. We'll head down to breakfast together."

Forty minutes later, when I walk into the kitchen with Avery, whatever ridiculous conversation the boys are having while eating their pancakes stops so fast it's like someone hit the mute button. Spencer, Matty, and Logan stare at us.

Were they talking about me instead of dissecting all six *Star Wars* episodes again? I walk toward an empty seat at the head of the table, facing the patio. Through the French door, I see Avery's dad watering hanging baskets of petunias. I inhale slowly and look around the table at the boys. I know they must be waiting for me to ask about the Call, but I lock eyes with Avery and the two of us pull out our chairs and sit down. I'm having a *My Fair Lady* moment. I'm the crass Eliza Doolittle and Avery is the gentlemanly Professor Higgins, struggling to turn me into a proper lady with good manners.

Avery passes me a service plate heaped with food.

"Pancakes? Sausage?"

"Thank you," I say, digging in.

"Can you pass that syrup?" Avery says.

"Sure." The tension builds, and I have to bite the inside of my cheek so I don't start laughing. Finally, Spencer breaks.

"Joey drunk dialed you last night!"

I pause. Calm Rosie is leaving the building.

"How would you know?" I'm talking to Spencer but glaring at Matty. "What did you tell them? This is private."

"They overheard me telling your parents."

"Telling my parents? What? Spill it, Matty." I'm so angry, I'm losing my appetite.

"Your parents said if Joey contacted you, I should tell them first. Then I should tell you."

I'm tired of feeling like I'm being handled, like I can't be trusted. I stab a breakfast link with my fork and speak as evenly as possible through clenched teeth. I don't need to make Avery's dad think I'm a freak by throwing a scream fest.

"Matty, if we were home right now, I swear to God I would throw this sausage right at your head." I wave the skewered meat to underscore my point.

A bug-eyed Logan reaches for my wrist and gently guides my fork-clutching hand back to the table.

"Give her the phone," Logan tells Matty.

"She's supposed to call her parents first."

"Give. Her. The. Phone," Logan repeats.

Matty's cheeks flush deeper than usual. Slowly and deliberately, he pushes back his chair, walks toward me, slams the phone down on the table, and exits through the patio door. Avery glances at me sympathetically, then follows Matty. Spencer leaves too. I'm not sure if it's because he's afraid of me or feels bad for Matty. He takes his plate with him, though.

"Joey left you a voice mail," Logan says. "It was three

o'clock in the morning New Jersey time. I think Spencer's probably right about it being a drunken call. But Matty didn't play the message for us. Swear."

He's holding up his right hand like he's taking an oath. I nod and stare down at my food. I feel humiliated. Tears sneak out the corners of my eyes and trickle down my jaw-line. Logan hands me a napkin and I quickly wipe my cheeks. Tentatively, Logan rests his hand on top of mine. His touch calms me down.

"You're lucky. You're getting this over with now. You only fall in love for the first time once."

"That's very Taylor Swift of you," I say. But Logan's right, and I feel better knowing he's trying to make me feel better.

Logan gives me a soft half smile and then he gets up from the table and walks outside. I watch him go and won-der when he first fell in love. Did his heart get broken or did he break some girl's heart? I pick up my phone and dial my voice mail. I punch in my four-digit code: Joey's birth-day. How lame am I?

"Yo, Rosie . . ." There's a long pause and I hear music and muffled speaking like he's covering the mouthpiece. "Call me." I play it two more times just to confirm he's being as big of a dick as I thought he was the first time I heard it. Yo, Rosie? I used to be "baby," and what's with the "yo"? So Joey thinks he's all street now? Yeah, right. He'd last two seconds away from his mommy.

I don't know what I was expecting from Joey, but it was definitely more. The thought of hearing Joey's voice again was so much better than the reality of Joey. At least he didn't mention Phoenix or the Fourth of July. Funny. He finally calls and I've got an excuse to talk to him, but somehow I know if I do, I'll be more of a loser than I already am. I've got to stop messing up. I text Lilliana instead. I tell her about Joey's call and ask if she's heard anything about my skanky ex and his jailbait girlfriend. Then I call my mom. Matty will be proud.

I don't even say hello when she picks up the phone. "He called," I say, and then I start to cry. "He's such a jerk."

"Aw, honey. Don't cry. He's not worth it. You didn't call him back, did you?" Mom says sympathetically.

"No. And I'm not going to, don't worry."

"I believe you. I think you should let the lawyer or his assistant know about this. I don't want that boy getting you in any more trouble. Do you want me to call Steve Justice?"

"It's okay. I'm supposed to talk to him today anyway."

"I miss you, honey. Do you want to come home?"

I wasn't expecting that. Yesterday I would have jumped at the offer. Today, after hearing Joey's voice, I'm not so sure. Lilliana is right. I need to see this trip through to the end. No, I'm right. I want to see this trip through to the end.

"I miss you too, Mom, but Matty would be disappointed. You know how sensitive he can be." *And so do I,* I think, feeling triple the guilt over my sausage-assault threat. "How's Dad? Is Eddie's job going okay?"

"They're both fine, *mija*."

"Can I talk to Pony? Is he around?"

"Of course he's around, where else would he be?" Mom chuckles. "Hold on. I'll put the phone up to his ear." After some shuffling around, I hear Mom's voice; it sounds as far away as she is. "Go ahead. He's listening."

"Pony? How's my good doggy? It's me, Rosie. I miss you, ya big pooch." As expected, he doesn't say anything. After a few seconds, Mom is back on the phone.

"He looks confused."

"I'll bet. Is Eddie taking him for walks?"

"What do you think? Your father takes him every morning and every night."

"Tell Dad and Eddie I love them."

"I will. Call me after you talk to Steve Justice."

"Okay, Ma. Love you."

"Love you too."

I walk outside and over to the pool house, where I find everyone sitting around watching a show involving catching very big fish. I plop myself on the couch next to Matty. He's got his arms crossed and he won't look at me. I take my phone and put it on his thigh and then I lean my head on his shoulder. He knows that means I'm sorry. I was wrong. But, after pointing a breakfast link at his head, I know I owe him more. I need to say this out loud, in front of everyone.

"I'm really sorry. I shouldn't have threatened you with the sausage."

Still nothing. I get up and stand between him and the television.

"You just did what my parents asked. I was wrong. And selfish."

That last part gets his attention.

"You were what?"

"Wrong! Is that what you want to hear?"

"Yes. And . . ."

"Selfish," I mumble. Matty's always teasing me about that, but I know there's a major grain of truth in his jokes.

We stare at each other for a full five seconds before

Avery pipes up. "Okaaay. Well, now that we got that out of the way, Rosie and I are going to get mani-pedis."

"Huh?" says Spencer.

"Nail stuff," Logan says.

"Can you boys manage on your own for a while?" Avery asks.

I jump in here. "Are you kidding? They've got a big day planned. First, the Book Depository where JFK was shot. Next, the ranch where, and I quote, 'they filmed the popular eighties, and recently revived, TV series *Dallas*.' Don't ask me how they even know that. And then it's on to the Museum of the American Railroad . . ."

Spencer is smiling all proud-like because he knows I've finally read his trip itinerary and committed it to memory. Avery is less pleased.

"That's it. We're going out to a club tonight. I want you to tell people y'all had fun when you visited me."

I'm smiling now. I like this girl, which is strange, because aside from Lilliana, I don't usually bond with girls very easily. And to think, I didn't want to spend two nights here. Now I'm so glad we are. But then I think about our line dancing outing in Nashville, and my mood plummets.

"Are we going to a country bar?" I ask.

"I said fun," Avery shouts, making me jump. "I want you to have fun. Not everyone in Texas wears cowboy hats and Wranglers and goes out boot scootin' on Friday nights."

I'm down with her frustration about unfair stereotypes. Not everyone in New Jersey is overly tanned and "stars" in asinine cable reality shows. The view from the New Jersey Turnpike isn't representative of the farms, beaches, and mountains that make up the other ninety-five percent of our state, and we don't all know people in the Mafia.

"I can't wait," I exclaim. Then I add, "Does your salon have that new kind of gel manicure?"

"They do! Cool colors, too," Avery says. "I may get my brows done as well; whataya say?"

"I'm in!"

I call Steve Justice's office while we're en route to the salon. Miranda answers. I fill her in about Joey's message and she puts me on the phone with Steve—that's what he tells me to call him. He's a pretty chill guy. I'm glad, because I probably would have giggled if I had to refer to him as Mr. Justice. It sounds like he's some twenty-first-century superhero. Steve asks me a bunch of questions about the night I torched Joey's car, and he tells me he's going to send an investigator out to talk with Joey's neighbors. This guy really goes the extra mile. I wonder what this is costing my dad. Then he puts Miranda back on the line.

"When are you due back in New Jersey?" she asks.

I can't even remember what day it is. Let me think—it's Tuesday, and I'll be flying home Sunday night on the red-eye.

"Uh, Monday?"

"Okay, I'll set up an appointment for you and your parents to come in and talk to Steve before your court date."

"By the way, you were right," I tell Miranda. "Steve says he's sending an investigator over to Joey's neighborhood."

"He's sending me," Miranda says, and I can tell I've touched a nerve. "He couldn't get his guy, so now I have to do it. I'm the investigator. I'm the paralegal. I'm the secretary. I do everything around here!" She yells that last part, for Steve's benefit, I'm guessing. I start to laugh.

"I'm serious," she says, but I can tell she's just busting Steve.

"I believe you."

"Anyway, it's best to have as much information as possible before your court appearance."

"Thank you," I say, and I really mean it. "Thanks for everything."

"We'll stay in touch."

* * *

Avery tells me she's hired a car to take us to a club tonight. At my house, we only use limos when we're going to the airport or prom. "It's picking us up at nine," she says. We're in her room, listening to music, drinking iced green tea, and getting ready to go out. It feels like a holiday.

I'm wandering around her room, looking at framed pictures of Avery's friends and family at various events, when a thick book on her nightstand catches my eye. I pick it up. It's Jimmy Carter's White House memoirs. In what universe would I find myself reading a book like this? In what universe do I read nonfiction books for fun?

"He inspired me to do Habitat for Humanity this summer," Avery says. "He's a great man."

"What will you be doing?"

"Spending a week building housing for families outside El Paso, Texas. Near the Mexican border."

I put the book down and look at Avery. She's wearing a denim mini with a blue halter that really makes her eyes pop, especially now that she's wearing contacts instead of glasses.

"Want me to do your hair?" I ask. I may not be able to build houses, but hair I can handle.

I give her blond locks some Jersey style and also do her makeup before I finish getting ready. It's so nice to be able to take my time. I wear a super-girly minidress with a tiny floral print, spaghetti straps, and a built-in bra that's surprisingly supportive, kind of like Avery turned out to be. And I love how my lavender finger- and toenails look against my olive skin. My hair is cascading past my shoulders and my smoky eyes would make *Seventeen*'s beauty editor proud. A spritz of perfume and I'm all set.

When we step outside, I instantly feel three sets of male eyes on us. We look good. But so do the guys. And they smell good too. Matty always cleans up nicely when he wants to and Spencer, well, his hair could still use some product, but he's not wearing a cartoon T-shirt, so that's a plus. And there's something about Logan in jeans and a snug-fitting tee that makes me want to see Logan without jeans and a snug-fitting tee. . . . I have to stop myself from reaching up and smacking my own head.

I whip out my disposable camera and take a few group shots before asking Matty to take one of just me and Avery in front of the fountain. A minute later, a black stretch limo pulls into the circular drive, and I feel all rock star when the driver gets out and opens the door for us.

"After you, girls," Matty says.

Avery and I link arms and we slide into the cavernous backseat. I'm so psyched to be all dressed up and on my way out. A very girly squeal is threatening to escape my mouth. I can't wait to see this club.

"The driver won't turn back into a mouse at midnight, will he?" I ask.

"Nope. He's ours until dawn." She pauses. "Wasn't the driver a horse?"

"That's right. How could I forget? Cinderella is my favorite princess."

"Me too!"

I'm so glad Avery's not one of those princess bashers. I mean, I know women are supposed to stand on their own and all. I get that. But every once in a while it doesn't hurt to wish for a fairy godmother, a little magic, and a happy ending.

Chapter 12

Avery asks the driver to drop us off a few blocks from the club. She doesn't say why, but I know that hiring a limo was her way of making things easier for her friends, not impressing people, even though she's pretty stinkin' rich. Lilliana would like her. I could see us expanding our twosome to a threesome if Avery lived in New Jersey. As we approach the club, I can hear the thump, thump, thumping of a bass beat and the crash of symbols every time the door swings open. Avery explains they have bands downstairs and a deejay and dance floor upstairs.

"It's all ages. They give out wrist bands if you're over twenty-one, but scoring alcohol is not impossible." Avery smiles. "Especially for us regulars."

I've already decided I'm not drinking. I need to hate

Joey for the foreseeable future and I don't want a warm fuzzy buzz to prompt my own drunk dial.

Without making a big deal about it, Logan pays for everyone's cover. Once inside, we negotiate the crowd as Avery leads us to a staircase at the back of the club. Upstairs, Avery, who indeed manages to score herself a light beer, pulls Logan onto the dance floor. It's a fast song and I watch them, wondering if she meant what she said about staying single—or if they'll wind up as a couple once they're both at ASU studying sustainability and saving the world together.

When the music slows, Avery turns toward us, but Logan pulls her back and puts his arm around her waist. My heart constricts for a millisecond and I hold my breath. My good mood is fading fast. I need to turn it around. Matty and Spencer are leaning on the bar drinking sodas. A diet Coke and those two? I love them, but that's not going to cut it. Instead of joining the guys, I head for the ladies' room to fix my lip gloss and regroup.

As I exit the restroom, I spot a pay phone at the end of the hallway. I rummage in my purse for that calling card. I'm not going to do anything crazy. I just need to hear a voice from home so I can shake off my jealousy and lift my spirits. I reread the instructions on the back of the card and dial Lilliana's number. It goes to voice mail. "Hey, it's me. Using the calling card you gave me. Okay. Call me later." She probably didn't recognize the number. No biggie.

I scan the club and find everyone standing together at the bar, where Avery appears to have snagged herself yet another beer. Interesting. But who am I to judge?

I shoulder my way across the crowded room and I'm about to scooch between these two girls standing near our group when I hear one girl say to the other with disdain: "*El comelibros* has been checking you out since he got here." I follow her gaze. She's looking at Spencer. No effin' way. She just called my Spence a bookworm! Actually, it's even more offensive. *Comelibros* literally means "eats books." Who does she think she is? Her friend answers in Spanish. Roughly translated, she's says Spencer needs to get over himself.

My pulse starts to race and my body gets hot. I can't help it. I lose it. I stick my face in theirs and say: *"No, tú tienes que olvidarlo. Algún dia él va a ser el próximo* Bill Gates. *Y de todas formas, él está conmigo!"* Basically, I tell her to get over herself, that Spencer's going to be the next Bill Gates, and anyway, he's with me. Then I barge between the two of them and join my friends.

"Bitch," one of them mumbles, again in Spanish, as I pass. I snap my head around and stare. "I heard you!"

She takes a step toward me, but her gal pal grabs her arm. Next thing I know, Logan is at my side. "Everything okay over here, *amiga?*" he asks.

"Fine." Then I take Spencer's hand and pull him to the dance floor. He looks confused as I drag him around, looking for a good spot—I want those bitches to see us.

"Why were you arguing about Bill Gates?" Spencer asks.

"Someone's gotta defend Microsoft." I shake my head in mock disbelief. "Apple groupies."

We're finally in a good area and Spencer is bopping to the music. It's a little like dancing with Elmo, but who cares. He's my friend.

"So, you're fluent in Spanish?"

"Not exactly. My mom is."

Spencer leans in and shouts over the music. "I'm taking Latin." His eyes are wide and innocent, and for the first time I notice that he's got killer lashes.

"That's cool." And I mean it. There is something very cool about the way Spencer knows what he likes and doesn't make any apologies for it. I feel bad for dismissing him and his Snoopy tee when we met and drooling over Logan's biceps. Spencer was there for me when Matty and I weren't speaking. I wish I could be more like Spencer and less like the girls who ragged on him. I'm relieved he didn't know what they said.

Matty, Logan, and Avery join us on the dance floor. Avery cups her hand over my ear. "You're not so selfish."

Avery speaks Spanish? Of course she does. Gotta be bilingual to save the world.

"I shouldn't have lost it like that. It's a pattern with me, in case you haven't noticed."

"You are a wild child," she says. "But you've got a good heart."

Do I? Avery does. That's for sure. I don't blame Logan for wanting to drive all this way to see her. Matty taps me on the shoulder and waves my phone at me.

"Text from Lilliana," he says.

I take my phone and read it. SORRY ABOUT BEFORE. DIDN'T RECOGNIZE THE NUMBER. BLONDIE BROKE UP W JOEY. So that's why he called me. WHEN? WHY? I type back. A reply comes a few seconds later. YESTERDAY. DUMPED HIM FOR A GUY W A CONVERTIBLE. CALL WHEN U CAN. LUV YA, BABE. I guess Joey's crispy 'Stang wasn't cutting it. I wonder what he's driving now. No. I don't wonder what he's driving.

Thoughts of Joey are not going to ruin my night.

I hand my phone back to Matty and start shimmying in front of him. Avery comes up and dances suggestively against his backside. He is loving life. I just hope he doesn't do that whoop, whoop thing with his hand and embarrass us all. But then I turn and Spencer's doing the very move I feared and I'm surprised to find I'm not mortified. Not even a little. I sidle up to Spence and bump his hip. He bumps me back. The music fills me from the inside out, making me feel like, well, I'm here with my friends. Deep in the heart of Texas. We dance together for at least five songs and then—

"Look out. Your BFFs. At five o'clock," Avery shouts. She twists my head in their direction. I should have known those girls weren't going to call me a bitch and let it drop. They plow through the crowded dance floor in their skinny jeans and tank tops complete with built-in power padding and head right toward me.

And then it happens. One of them—the one who's wearing entirely too many fuchsia sequins—checks me with her shoulder, hard. They slide over and start dancing with Logan and Matty. As if. I whirl around, about to grab the one who bumped me, but drop my hand to my side instead.

165

"What am I doing?" I whisper.

Avery comes to my rescue—all five-foot one of her. She hands me her beer (how many does that make?) and muscles her way between Matty and my attacker. Before I can stop her, Avery turns her back to the girl and nudges her with her hip, smiling the whole time. I get the feeling she's not quite sober.

"Yo. I was dancin' here," says the girl.

"That's right, you were," Avery yells over her shoulder.

Uh-oh. Things get positively messy after that. The bedazzled one's friend, who is dancing near Logan, turns to Avery, grabs both her shoulders, and pushes her. I was trying to avoid a fight, but I can't let her treat Avery that way. I put on my game face, walk up to the girls, and scream, "Back off!"

That's when one of them slaps me across the face. My skin stings, and I don't know how I keep it together, but I follow the golden rule of kindergarten and keep my hands to myself. Avery, however, does not. She slaps the girl right back, and that's when someone yells, "Girl fight!"

Out of the corner of my eye, I see two burly bouncers sweeping people out of their paths as they descend on the dance floor and hone in on us. Logan sees them too and at that point, he bends down and flings Avery over his shoulder. Matty sizes me up, hesitates, and grabs my hand instead. We dash toward the stairs, away from the bouncers and the dance floor, while the girls follow, swiping at me like two cats. On the first floor, we pass through the crowd in a blur, crash through the exit, and trip onto the sidewalk. The bouncers stop their pursuit at the door; they've got us where they wanted us anyway, I suppose. The five of us run down the street toward our waiting car. The sparkle sisters curse us up and down, complete with obscene hand gestures, but seem reluctant to pursue us in their stilettos. At least they got thrown out too.

The driver opens the back door as we approach the limo and tumble inside, all of us out of breath. Avery is the first to start giggling. One by one we join in until we're all belly laughing. Logan's eyes are tearing, he's laughing so hard. I didn't know that boy had it in him. It's nice to see. He looks younger.

"I've never been in a bar fight before," Avery gasps. "What an adrenaline rush!" Then she falls over onto Matty's lap. Matty looks surprised, but not unhappy. He lays a hand on her arm and goes with it.

"I'm sorry, everyone," I say. I feel like a shit. I've got

smart, classy Avery bitch slapping people in bars. I keep promising myself I'll be a better daughter, a better friend, a better person, but it's not working out so well. "I should have kept my mouth shut."

"Are you kidding? That's the most fun I've ever had," Spencer says. He's so serious, it makes my insides ache.

"Your heart was in the right place," Logan whispers.

He puts his arm around me and gives me a squeeze that sends a warm sensation right down to my toes. I have the urge to fall against him and sink into his side; I want both his arms around me. I want to feel like I'm part of a couple again. But instead, for a reason I don't completely understand, I shrug him off and lean toward the door to look out the window. The Dallas skyline rises sharply out of the flat landscape. *Just like Oz,* I think.

"I was trying to be better." I whisper to myself, but Logan hears.

"Give yourself a break," he says softly. "You're better than you think, Rosalita."

Oh, man, do I love the way my name sounds when Logan says it. In all the time we were together, Joey never said it. Not once. Then Logan takes my hand and gives my fingers a quick squeeze. When he makes a move to let go, I don't let him, and he doesn't seem to mind. By the time we cruise up the long driveway to Avery's estate, I'm feeling better. No, more than that, excited. Tomorrow, when my coach turns into a Taurus, I'll be ready for New Mexico, ready to kick impulsive/angry/reckless Rosie to the curb and own the rest of this road trip.

The sun is barely up and Logan is putting our bags in the trunk of the car. We all could have used more sleep, but Roswell is eight hours from here and the guys want to stop in Amarillo first to see something called Cadillac Ranch, which is going to add at least another hour to today's driving time. Avery's dad got up extra early to make us all a big breakfast. He's the best. I've got to send this family a fruit basket as a thank-you when I get home. We never did meet Avery's mom. I guess being a big-time cardiac surgeon doesn't allow for much time at home. I feel bad for Avery, and for her mom.

When it's time to say good-bye, I can't believe how choked up I get. I hug Avery, holding on to her slight shoulders for a beat too long.

"Thank you. For everything," I say, trying not cry.

"Thank you. For one crazy night. Come see me at ASU," she says. "Anytime."

"I will."

"Who knows? Maybe you'll love it and apply."

I never even considered that I'd be visiting ASU at the end of this trip. I guess because, until now, I didn't have any interest in touring some college campus, especially one that's so far away from New Jersey.

I smile at her. "New Jersey's beaches are the best in the summertime. You may need a break after building all those houses."

"You may just see me," she says.

I hope I do see Avery again—even if it is because she's Logan's girlfriend. Or Matty's. I'll be okay with that. I think. Why couldn't Spencer have shed his nerdiness and swept Avery off her feet? He deserves a girl like her.

I climb into the backseat with Matty. As we pass the fountain, he hands me my phone. "A text from Lilliana. It must be from last night. I guess I didn't notice it during the melee."

I look at the screen. BTW, JOEY KNOWS YOU'RE GOING TO ARIZONA.

Oh, shit. I guess I really did text him in my Benadryl haze. The fact that I racked up another TRO violation is nothing compared with my bigger worry. He wouldn't come after me, would he? I don't say a word, but Matty asks the question that's making the pancakes in my stomach feel like they're looking for a quick escape route.

"How did Joey find out about our trip?"

Chapter 13

I'm standing in a cow pasture along Interstate 40 in Amarillo, Texas, gaping at ten vintage Cadillacs buried nose down in the brown earth. The cars are covered in spray paint and graffiti. I snap a picture with my cheesy camera in a box.

"Awesome. This looks like Stonehenge," Matty says, shielding his eyes from the glare of the bright white sky as he looks up at the Cadillacs.

"Stonehenge is circular," Spencer says. "This is a straight line."

"It's basically crappy old cars in the dirt," I say. "We took a detour for this? Really?"

"There are no detours on a road trip, Catalano. There is only the road trip itself," Logan says. I'm momentarily bummed that I'm back to Catalano, but then he gives my upper arm a gentle squeeze and my stomach does a back handspring. But my mind reprimands my gut in an attempt to crush the oncoming crush. I throw in some sarcasm for good measure.

"Thank you, Deepak Chopra. What's next, yoga?" I snipe.

"Ha! Rosie doing yoga. An even more improbable sight than Cadillacs in the desert," Matty says. "You do know yoga is a form of exercise, not a cartoon bear, right?"

"Shut up, Matty."

"What? You know I'm right."

He is. He always is. It's like traveling through life with a six-foot Jiminy Cricket looking over my shoulder. Maybe I should think about joining a gym when I get back home. A gym with a pool. I like to swim, and I need to find a better way to deal with stress and my misplaced aggression, as Lilliana would put it. I'm feeling more than a little edgy right now. I've been trying to piece together my last communication with Joey. Did I text him and delete the evidence? Did I e-mail him in my antihistamine delirium? Probably not. I hardly ever use e-mail anymore, but I wish I had used Avery's laptop to check when I had the chance. Maybe it's just a coincidence. Joey could have found out where I'm headed from one of Eddie's friends. But Joey isn't the only thing that's got me all uptight. It's cloudy today, and during the entire ride across Texas, I could not stop scanning the horizon for tornados. Tornados and Wile E. Coyote. I watch those storm-buster shows on cable all the time, and this looks like the perfect place for one to touch down and siphon me, the boys, and the Taurus into its deadly cone.

When some actual tumbleweeds passed in front of the car, I made the mistake of wondering aloud if they come from one particular plant. Spencer, armed with a phone that is even smarter than he is, looked it up for me. Most tumbleweeds are just that, weeds called *Salsola* that were brought to North America in seed shipments from Asia. "So, a tumbleweed is nothing special, just a plant that dries out, disengages from its roots, and rolls away," he said while reading his screen.

A common weed, disengaged from my roots and blowing across America. It's exactly how I feel.

Now Mr. Smarty-pants moves on and is boring us with the details of these junkyard cars. "They are buried at the same angle as the Cheops pyramids," Spencer notes.

"Oh, here we go. Can we be done now, please?" I beg.

"Not before we take some pictures and use these."

Matty holds up two cans of spray paint. "Someone must have left them behind."

"So what? We're supposed to decorate the Cadillacs?" I ask.

"Of course," Spencer says. "That's why we're here."

Matty tosses a can to Spencer and starts shaking the other. The metal ball clanks as he walks over to one of the cars and writes his initials. Spencer sprays some ancient-looking design that probably has something to do with the origins of the universe. Logan takes the can from his brother and draws the recycling symbol, then tosses the can to me. I'm impressed they've all resisted any wisecracks about me lighting these babies on fire.

"Whatcha gonna do, Rosie? How're you gonna leave your mark?" Matty asks.

The way Matty says it makes me stop and really think about it. I'll probably never come this way again, honestly, because hello, why would I want to? But how will I leave my mark? I shake the can and mull it over as I walk toward one of the cars. Whatever I decide to paint here might be gone soon anyway. I think about my brick at Graceland, point the can, and spray.

"Hey, Matty! Can you take a picture of me?" I ask.

He walks over with my phone, points, and clicks, capturing Me at Cadillac Ranch standing next to a junk car, on which I've spray painted a big WHY? Those three letters cover a lot of territory for me. Next time I find myself in Amarillo, I intend to have some answers.

Logan walks over and takes a look. "Now who's going all Buddha on us?" And then he turns down the dirt road toward our car, making that round-up motion with his finger. Is it possible I'm getting used to just how annoying he can be?

The bulk of the drive from Amarillo to Roswell is spent on two highways—US 60 and US 70. I am bored and hungry and use my time to make some calls. First, my parents. Steve Justice called them to set up a prehearing meeting. Then Lilliana. No new Joey news, but she digs the photo I send of me at Cadillac Ranch.

I'm still antsy.

"I think I'm gonna call Avery," I announce.

"I texted her a few minutes ago," Matty says.

"You did?" Me and Spencer practically gasp in unison.

"Yeah. She says 'hi, ya'll,'" Matty says, doing his best Avery impersonation.

Logan remains silent, but I see his eyes shift toward

Matty in the rearview mirror. Is Logan jealous? Am I? And if I am, is it because Matty likes Avery or is it because Logan is jealous that Avery may like Matty? Then I wonder, if I jump out of this moving Taurus, will I die or simply tumble across the barren landscape like a *Salsola* plant?

I don't feel like calling Avery anymore even though it's possible I'm feeling most possessive of my new connection with her at this moment. I lean my head against the window, look across the endlessly flat landscape, and hope for a twister to take me away.

At some gas station in the middle of Nowheresville, the guys decide it's my turn to pump the gas. People can say all the snarky things they want about New Jersey, but at least we don't pump our own gas. All our stations are full service. It's the law and a good one if you ask me. Consequently, when I step out of the car and approach the pump, I realize I have no freakin' idea how to put gas in this car. I take out my emergency credit card and read the directions on the pump. I decide to get the gas cap off first. I twist and I twist, but it keeps making this awful crunching noise. I peek in the driver's-side window for some help and all three guys are laughing at me.

"I can't get the cap off. It's making funny noises," I whine.

"That usually indicates you're turning it the wrong way," Logan answers.

Spencer offers his contribution: "Lefty loosey, righty tighty."

I roll my eyes at them.

"There it is. The eye roll," Logan says.

"Pay up," Matty hoots. "I bet them five bucks you wouldn't get through this without an eye roll."

I flip them the bird. "What's that worth?" I say, and then sashay back to the pump.

Once I've got the filling process under control, the boys go into the Kwik Mart to buy drinks and snacks.

"Get me a Yoo-hoo! And some Cheez-Its." Nobody answers me. I do miss Avery. I should have called her earlier. I realize how much talking I don't do when I'm with Logan, Matty, and Spencer. I don't get most of their geek-centric pop culture references, and they don't bother to include me in their discussions anyway. It's either that or they all turn on me and it becomes Let's Tease Rosie time. It's getting old. I need to go on the offensive.

When they get back in the car (with Cheese Tidbits, ugh—everyone knows they suck), I take the lead on the conversation and play this game I learned in my high school theater class. It was either that or public speaking, so I picked the nicer teacher who never gives anyone less than a B.

"So, if you were a vegetable, what kind would you be and why?"

Spencer points to himself. "Am I supposed to answer that?" He's sitting in the back with me.

"We all are. It's an acting exercise. We'll take turns. You go first."

"Uh, okay. Let me think."

But Matty doesn't give him a chance. "I'd be an extra-large zucchini. For obvious reasons."

"Really. You see yourself walking around looking like a giant dick?" Logan asks.

"Yep," Matty agrees.

"Guys! Come on. Don't be gross."

"I'd be broccoli," Spencer decides.

"Okay, good. Why?" I ask. I'm happy Spencer is taking this seriously.

"Because I like broccoli."

I look out my window. This is not going the way I hoped.

I try again. "Maybe this would be more interesting if we let everyone else decide what kind of vegetable we are and why."

"Just vegetables?" Matty asks.

"Fine. We can do fruit too," I say. Maybe they'll find that easier. "Okay, so if I were a fruit, what kind would I be?"

Logan doesn't hesitate. "Bananas."

"Why?" I don't know why I'm bothering to ask.

"Uh, lemme think. Oh yeah, restraining order."

I'm not going to let him get to me. "Matty?"

"Um, strawberry."

"Why?"

"Because you were obsessed with Strawberry Shortcake lip gloss when you were in first and second grade. You had that massive collection you kept in a shoe box under your bed."

I can't believe he remembered that. I need a second before I speak again.

"Spencer? What would I be?"

"An orange."

I raise an eyebrow. This I have to hear.

"Because . . . I like oranges?" I offer.

"No. Because you're tough on the outside but sweet on the inside."

Whoa. Caught off guard again. I clear my throat to make those sneaky tears dissolve.

"Did the estrogen level just go up a notch, or am I

imagining it?" Logan asks. He starts coughing like he can't breathe. "Open the windows."

Who's the zucchini now? I don't let Logan's teasing bother me. I catch Spencer's eye and mouth "thank you." He winks and smiles. Spencer is neither a fruit nor a vegetable, more like the surprise toy in a box of healthy cereal.

Hours later, after crossing the Texas–New Mexico border at Farwell, I start seeing signs for the Flying Saucer McDonald's in Roswell. It looks awesome. Plus, I'm starving and I'm craving something, anything, dunked in ketchup.

"We are so there!" I nearly poke Spencer on the nose when I lean across him and point to the billboard on his side of the car. Logan just gives me his Logan look.

"What? They've got salads," I tell him.

"Screw the salad. A super-size meal and a shake, that's what I'm talking about," Matty says.

"Thank you!" I shout.

"Fine," Logan says.

We pull into the parking lot a short time later. The restaurant does indeed look like a flying saucer and the play area looks like a spaceship.

"Amazing." I sigh.

"Gee, Catalano," Logan says. "It's nice to see you're finally excited about something. After fifteen hundred miles, I was beginning to think we were boring you."

"Let's see what it looks like inside," I say. I'm the first one out of the car.

I walk through the gleaming silver door and head for the high-ceilinged play area. I smile up at Ronald and Grimace in space suits. If I only had to see fast-food-related kitschy alien stuff while we're in Roswell, I'd be a happy girl. But I know all about Spencer's bigger plans this afternoon.

We grab our food and sit down. I'm a little disappointed that this seating is normal McDonald's style.

"I was hoping this would be more like eating in a space-ship," I say out loud to no one in particular. I dip a fry in one of the five ketchup-filled mini-containers I've lined up on my tray like tequila shots.

"What? You thought we'd enter an antigravitational chamber and float around while we scarfed down burgers and fries?" Spencer asks. Coming from anyone else, this would be sarcasm. But Spencer really wonders if that's what I expected.

"Nah. I just thought the tables and chairs would be cooler."

"Word," Spencer says.

Spencer saying "word" has the same effect on me as my mother wearing my clothes. I take a sip of my milk shake to avoid smiling.

"Let's go," Logan says. "We have time to see the museum before it closes."

"Phew, that's a relief," I say. I buy myself some cookies on the way out. Tours make me hungry. Road trips make me hungry. Restraining orders and ex-boyfriends make me hungry. I think Logan has a point about emotional eating.

The International UFO Museum and Research Center in Roswell has a movie-theater-style marquis out front. THE TRUTH IS HERE, it brags. Doubt it. Inside we are greeted by an alien in chinos holding a sign that says WELCOME . . . PLEASE SIGN IN AND ENJOY YOUR VISIT. Again, I'm gonna have to go with "doubt it." Admission's only five bucks, but one glance around tells me even that is a waste of money. They offer an audio tour, like the kind we did at Graceland, but the museum's really only one big room with bulletin board exhibits like "The Roswell Incident Timeline" or "The Great Cover-up." I don't want to walk around and read yellowed newspaper clips.

"You know what this reminds me of?" Spencer asks.

"The *Deep Space Nine* when Quark, Rom, and Nog travel

back in time to a twentieth-century Roswell?" Matty offers.

Spencer and Matty fist bump each other. Nerds of a feather. At least Spencer didn't say "word" this time.

Logan looks at me. "We've got to get those two laid." His conspiratorial smile gives me the shivers. That dimple is going to do me in.

"Don't look at me!" I say. I need air. "I'll be in the gift shop. Come find me when you're done."

After a quick look around at the alien-theme souvenirs, I decide there's absolutely nothing I want to buy—one more bizarre occurrence in Roswell. I never go shopping and come back empty-handed. I leave the poor excuse for a gift shop, find Matty, and ask him for my phone.

"Here," he says. "Why don't you just hold it for the rest of the trip? I won't tell. I can use a break from your parents' incessant communications."

Matty doesn't have anything to worry about. Joey's drunk call extinguished my burning need to communicate with him. I find a spot by the museum entrance and sit down. Something is shifting inside me. My homesickness has abated at the moment; now I'd rather be in New Mexico staring at a plastic alien than on my way back to New Jersey to face what I did.

I pick up a brochure about the museum and leaf through it. Lilliana's text about Joey knowing where I am is still bothering me. Joey wouldn't actually show up in Phoenix, would he? How would he know how to find me? I don't want to talk to the guys about it, especially Logan. He's no longer looking at me like I'm the crazy girl crashing his road trip, and I don't want to ruin that.

Finally, I call my parents for my daily check-in (Pony didn't want to come to the phone this time) and text Lilliana. My stomach feels queasy when she texts me about some party at our friend Xavier's. She took Marissa with her. Would I have gone if I were there? Probably not. The last time I went to a party, well—fire, TRO. Enough said. But what about the next party? What's the rest of my summer going to be like when I get back?

A few minutes later I get another text. I figure it's from Lilliana again, but I'm shocked by what I see. CAN WE TALK? Here I just got done telling myself that Matty had nothing to worry about. It's from Joey.

The next five minutes is like being on a crash diet with a plate of chocolate brownies in front of me. It's a struggle, but in the end, I dial Avery for support.

"Help me. I just got a text from Joey."

"Be strong, girl. What'd he say?"

"He wants to talk."

"Have his attorney call your attorney," Avery says.

"I wish you were here. We're at the UFO museum."

From where I'm sitting I can see all three boys. They're meandering around sporting dorky headsets—that are no doubt filling their heads with all kinds of fascinating facts—and checking out the uninspired displays. I explain the scene to Avery.

"Did those guys not understand what I meant about having fun?"

"Be glad you missed Matty and Spencer's *Deep Space Nine* discussion."

"Matty asked me for my number."

"We know." I tense up waiting to hear what she says next.

"He's a sweet guy; I would have felt bad saying no. But I don't want to lead him on. Distance and timing are not in his favor."

"I can relate." My muscles relax.

"Ya know, Rosie, sometimes when you don't know what to do, it's okay to do nothing."

I think about that as I delete Joey's text.

⚹ ⚹ ⚹

Later, at the motel, I tell Matty about the Joey text and give him my phone. "Turn it off. Lock it in your suitcase. I'm tired of looking at it."

"I wish I could, but Mama Catalano would not survive a communications blackout," Matty says.

I sigh and grab my toothbrush. "I'm going to bed." Exhaustion and sheer boredom are overtaking me. We drove such a long way for old cars and little green men. Thank God for the McDonald's spaceship, lackluster seating and all, or today would have been a total bust. It's not that I don't want to have fun on this trip; it's just that this stuff is not my idea of a good time. I feel like I'm on a field trip. A loooong field trip.

I fall into bed with Matty without a fuss. I merely plop a pillow between us, turn on my side, and mutter, "The Grand Canyon better not be the bland canyon. I hope that hole in the ground rocks my world."

"No pun intended?" Matty says.

I open the eye that's not smushed against my pillow. "We've been spending too much time together," I mumble as I shut it again and drift off to sleep.

Chapter 14

The next morning I'm awakened by a bright light.
My eyes flutter open and there's a glowing white orb about
two inches from my face. Is that the sun? Or . . . oh no.
I gingerly feel the back of my head and neck. Phew. No
probes. That's a relief. Because obviously, if anyone's getting abducted while we're in Roswell, it's me. That's the
kind of luck I have. Reassured, I slowly reach toward the
light—and burn myself.

"Sonavabitch!!!" It *is* two inches from my face, and so
are the guys.

I sit straight up in bed and grab my sizzling index finger. It better not blister.

"What the hell? Why are you idiots shining the desk
lamp in my eyes? A bunch of freakin' weirdos. That's who

I'm seeing America with. A bunch of freakin' weirdos."

"There's the Rosie we love," Matty says.

"Don't be mad, Rosie. We have a surprise for you," Spencer says.

"I know, I know. Area 51. More alien crap," I huff.

"Nope. Change of plans. We're going off the itinerary." Spencer sounds so proud of himself.

"Wait, we're not going to Carlsbad Caverns, are we?" I'd seen signs for it on the interstate. "I am so not doing any more caves."

"Better," Logan says. He's already dressed and zipping up his duffel bag.

"You're putting me on the first plane home?"

"It's a surprise," Matty says. He's waving around a brochure that he must have gotten from the table in the lobby. If you can call the Formica counter with the cash register, plastic plant, and Mr. Coffee a lobby.

"Let me see that." I stand on top of the bed and lunge for the brochure. Matty, who is now standing next to me, dangles it two feet above my head. I grab hold of his arm to steady myself and try to launch myself to grab it. It's no use. Jolly Green is too tall.

I'm about to make one more attempt, but as soon as

I'm in motion, Matty kicks my legs out from under me. I fall back onto the bed and take him down. Now he's sprawled on top of me, grinning. We've wrestled like this since we were kids, but for some reason, I'm blushing from head to toe. My embarrassment is embarrassing, but my bigger concern is the fact that I didn't sleep in a bra and I'm worried, well . . . let's just leave it at that. I'm worried.

"Get off me, you big oaf." I'm beginning to sweat.

Spencer looks at us with his hands on his hips. "I'd say get a room, but—"

"Enough! Somebody better tell me where we're going today," I demand as Matty rolls over.

"Albuquerque," Logan says.

"To do what?"

"You'll just have to wait," Matty says. He stands up, folds the brochure, and puts it in his back pocket. "This is gonna be so cool."

"Does it involve bathing suits and suntan lotion?" I ask.

"Nope," Logan says. "Jeans and . . . do you even own athletic shoes?"

"Yes. I just don't have running shoes. And what's up with the glasses?" *Thick* glasses, at that. They make his eyes look itty bitty. "I never saw you wear them before."

"Wouldn't you opt for contacts if your glasses looked like that?" Spencer says. "You should have seen him when he was fat and wore glasses. Attractive. Very attractive."

"I'd kick your ass, little bro, but we don't have time," Logan jokes.

Discovering Logan was fat and wears glasses makes something click in my brain. Sure, Logan's got a confident, borderline cocky attitude, but it's more about being smart, and right, than about being hot. Meanwhile, Joey knows exactly how good he looks and works it—flirting with the world is Joey's modus operandi. Logan, on the other hand, knows he's smart, but he doesn't necessarily know how good looking he is. "It explains a lot," I blurt out.

"What?" Logan asks.

"Nothing," I say. "Gotta get ready."

Thankfully he does the guy thing and moves on.

"You've got a half hour, Catalano. Remember, jeans. No shorts."

Forty-five minutes later, we're back in the Taurus. Yes, I took a little longer getting ready today. The round brush was working its magic as I blew my hair dry, and I did not want to rush the process. For once, nobody complains. Logan even lets me ride shotgun.

"You look . . . nice," Logan says softly as he opens the door for me.

I'm not sure whether I should return the compliment or check the back of his neck for probes.

"Thanks," I say. Best to keep it simple.

I click my seat belt and stare out the window. Spencer fires up his tunes. It's his turn to pick the music. I put my shades on, close my eyes, and listen to his first selection. Make that *try* to listen. Classic rock. Better than country, but with Spencer strumming along on the acoustic, it's like being forced to watch someone play Guitar Hero.

"Can we listen to my songs next?" I ask. It's worth a shot.

"That's depends," Matty says.

"On what?"

"If you have an appropriate playlist," Logan says.

"My Bruce mix includes 'Badlands,'" I offer.

"There are no badlands in New Mexico," Spencer explains.

"There is no *Kansas* in New Mexico. And yet that's what I find myself listening to," I say. "'Dust in the Wind'? Does it get any sadder?"

Spencer defends his choice. "I'm learning this guitar part."

I know I'm difficult, I'm aware of that. But these three have no idea how utterly infuriating they can be in their collective passive-aggressive way. I sigh and accept my defeat.

As we pull onto Route 40 west, I look out the window at the caramel-colored landscape. I swear we've passed that same mountain ten times already and we've only been in the car for eleven minutes. My impatience grows with every mile until I blurt out to no one in particular, "If you're not going to tell me where we're going, can you at least tell me how long it's going to take to get there?"

"Three hours," Matty says.

Why do I bother asking? Deflated, I sink down in my seat. Every time we get in this car, it seems like I always spend a minimum of three hours with my butt on these taupe fabric seats until our next destination. I'm getting tired of leaving Somewhere, driving through the Middle of Nowhere, and ending up Somewhere again. I click the heels of my Skechers together. Nothin'. Must only work with ruby slippers. Either that, or my heart knows I don't really want to go home.

We've traveled nearly two hundred miles and for the past hour, no one has said a word. This would never happen in a car full of girls. We'd have endless topics of conversation: movies, boys, music, SATs, celebrity gossip, boys, split ends, gel manicures. Whatever. Girls can fill the silence.

"Why does it take so long to get anywhere?" I finally say.

"It's a big country, Catalano," Logan offers.

"That's why my family sticks to the edges."

"Quit your constant complaining," Matty says. "We're here."

"Really? Where?" I perk up and look out the window.

"I think the sign says it all," Logan says.

"Sandia Stables?" I'm smiling 'cause I know.

"We decided that the only thing better than seeing an alien in New Mexico would be seeing you on horseback," Matty chimes in. "I told them how you've always wanted to ride a horse."

"Seriously?" My eyes and nose burn with happy tears, and for few seconds, that's all I can manage to say. Finally, I clear my throat and speak.

"Thank you, guys. This is awesome."

If I had known, I would have worn the cowgirl tank I bought in Nashville. It seems like that was a month ago. We drive down the long dirt road leading to the horse ranch. Logan parks near the barn and we all get out of the car.

"This one is on me," Logan says, and reaches for his wallet.

I am positively giddy and have to restrain myself from jumping up and down when I see my horse emerge from the barn with the rancher. She is beautiful, just like the copper-colored pair I saw on the ridge in Virginia. She has a diamond-shaped white spot between her deep brown eyes and her mane hangs between her ears like horsey bangs; how adorable.

"Okay now, miss. Why don't you step on over here and I'll show you how to git up on Penny?"

Aw, her name is Penny. It reminds me of Pony. Wait until I tell him about this. As I walk toward Penny and the ranch man, I'm suddenly anxious. Does Penny know I'm nervous? Aren't horses supposed to be really good at sensing human emotion? I've seen *The Horse Whisperer* on AMC. I want her to like me.

"Take a deep breath and relax," the rancher says. "That's my first rule."

In through the nose, out through the mouth. "I'm good."

"Okay now. You're going to stand on the left side of the horse. Take the reins in your left hand, and put that hand up here by the horse's mane."

I follow his directions.

"Good. Now, without letting go of the reins, grab on to her mane."

I'm worried about hurting Penny, but I listen. He's the expert.

"Okay, now you're going to use your right hand to turn the stirrup toward you. Good. That's it. Now put your left foot in there."

Right hand. Left foot. *Okay, pardner, I'm still with you.*

"There ya go. Now grab the back of the saddle, give a little bounce on the ball of your right foot, and pull on her mane and the saddle until you get yourself up in the stirrup on your left."

I never turn around to look at the boys. I just concentrate, bounce, pull, and whoa! Here I am, almost on the horse.

"That a girl. Now swing that right foot over and you're there."

Plop. Houston, I am in the saddle. The stirrups are higher than I expected. I thought my legs would hang down more.

"Whatever you do. Do not let go of the reins. Got it?" Mr. Sandia Stables says.

I give him a toothy smile. I'm quivering inside. "Got it."

Could it be that I'm a natural? That wasn't hard at all. Ha! Look at me. Giddyap. I'm grinning proud. And here's the better part: Logan, Matty, and Spencer all make complete asses of themselves trying to mount their horses. It's beyond me how Matty, who's almost as tall as his horse, can't seem to pull himself up smoothly.

"Grab the back of the saddle, not the horn," the rancher yells. "This isn't a carousel."

I think Matty's horse doesn't like him. It keeps shaking its head and razzing him. It takes Matty at least three tries before his long, skinny leg finally swings up and over. Spencer gets up on the first try but collapses on the horse's neck before getting his right leg in the proper position. Logan's horse keeps taking one step away every time he goes to put his foot in the stirrup. Finally, the ranch guy holds the reins and stirrup for him. I'm surprised he didn't boost Logan up and over too. Now, that would have been priceless.

"All right," says the rancher. "Now that we've got you all in the saddle, I'll teach you basic starting and stopping, and then my son, Lucca, over there is going to take you out on the trail."

I follow the rancher's finger to where he's pointing. Well, would you look at Lucca. That tush was made for Wrangler's. I'm itching to fluff my hair, but it's like the ranch man reads my inner monologue.

"I said it before, but this bears repeating. Never drop the reins," says the father of Lucca. Lucca the god. "Keep your backs straight and your heels down. Eyes up. Don't look at the ground. You look at the ground, you'll be on the ground."

We snap into our best posture and follow directions as the rancher continues.

"Now for some horseback riding one-zero-one. Keep the reins in the center of the saddle, by the horn. Move the reins to the left, and your horse will go left; move them to the right, and the horse will go right. Pull back, slowly, not with a quick jerk, and the horse will stop. To get the horse walking, squeeze with your calves and the horse will go. As you feel more comfortable, I'd like you to try to guide the horse by using that same technique. To move left, apply pressure with your calf to the horse's right side and vice versa."

"Do we have to say giddyap?" Why'd I ask that?

"Only if you think that's going to give you a fuller experience, miss." Rancher sarcasm.

"You'll have to excuse her," Matty says. "She's from New Jersey."

"So are you guys!"

"Yes, but we don't try quite as hard to make it obvious." Logan laughs.

"Yeah, well, maybe I don't think it's something to be ashamed of," I snipe.

That's it. I squeeze with my calves and Penny starts walking. All on her own, she moseys away from the barn toward the nearest trail and I don't try to stop her. That's my girl. Just get me away from these idiots. We understand each other, me and Penny.

"Hold up, little lady," Father of Lucca calls after me. "Don't head down the trail without Lucca."

I wave over my shoulder and play dumb. Let Lucca catch me. Let them all catch me. I can't wait until Penny is galloping. I hear a commotion behind me as the guys attempt to put their horsies in drive.

"Watch it," I hear Logan yell.

"Uh, space, Matty. I need room to turn," Spencer says.

I smile and let Penny take her time as we amble toward

the woods. Then comes the cloppity-clop of a horse coming up quickly behind me. I watch the butt of Lucca pass me on the left. His flexed thigh muscles sure look nice as he pulls in front of me and spins his horse around to face Penny. He nods and tips a straw cowboy hat at me. I glance behind me to see the boys have finally achieved forward motion and are closing the gap between us.

"You're a feisty one, aren't ya?" Lucca says.

"I'm just excited. This is my first time on a horse."

"Well, I'd say you're doing fine so far."

"Thanks." It feels nice to be spoken to this way by a boy. No taunting. No irony in his voice.

"You like horses?" Lucca asks.

"I do. And I really like Penny. I think she gets me." I stroke her mane and pat her neck. I think I feel her smiling.

"Looks like it," Lucca says.

Oh, man, I love his five o'clock shadow and the way the little indent at the base of his neck provides the perfect cradle for the turquoise and silver charm that hangs from his leather choker. I can't say that I've ever had a cowboy fantasy, but that just changed. I'm mulling over a way to surreptitiously get a pic of Lucca's Wrangler butt on horseback when the guys finally join us.

"We all here?" Lucca asks. "Let's go, then. Why don't you ride behind me, pretty lady? The rest of you follow in single file."

Pretty lady. I know he probably says that to all the girls, but it's something I don't hear very often, and by "very often" I mean ever. I sit taller.

Our horses mosey up the trail a bit as we follow Lucca's instructions and stay in single file. It's already pretty hot—not steamy New Jersey hot, more like standing in an oven hot—and our rides don't appear to be in any rush. Both Penny and I could use another application of deodorant. The view is nice, though, and I'm not just talking about Lucca's gluteus maximus.

We ride in relative silence. I say "relative" because me and Lucca aren't talking and Logan, who is immediately behind me, is not saying a word, but I can hear Matty and Spencer yapping away in the back. Words like "indigenous" and "vegetation" drift my way and I have to roll my eyes. Most of the trees on the trail look like run-of-the-mill evergreen. Nothing too unfamiliar except that I notice when I breathe in, and this is going to sound weird, I can smell them. The air smells so clean. I feel like one of those women in an air freshener commercial. Back home, I'd never give trees or other plants or how they smelled a second thought. Lucca stops and lets me and Penny catch up. I stare beyond the tree line at the jagged tops of the gray mountains. Lucca follows my gaze.

"The Sandia Mountains," he says. He looks older than all of us; around twenty, I'm guessing.

"Thus the name of your stables."

"Correct."

"What kind of trees are these?" For some reason, I care all of a sudden.

"Firs and spruce. A few ponderosa here and there; nothing too special," he says. "You've probably got these in Jersey."

"New Jersey," I say. I can't help it. He's touched a sore spot. In my opinion, you can only call it "Jersey" if you live in Jersey.

"New Jersey," Lucca corrects.

"You don't hear me dropping the 'new' from your state, do you? Where would that get us, huh?"

"Cancún?" Lucca gives me a half smile. "Just like I thought. Feisty."

I smile too. Partly because I'm picturing shirtless Lucca surrounded by sand and turquoise water, the scent of coconut suntan lotion on his skin and . . . I'm going to fall off Penny if I go on. I shake my head to snap out of it. "Well, it's just that I hate when people who aren't from my state do that—especially Philly sports fans."

"I stand corrected."

"Except you're sort of sitting right now," I tease.

I don't know why I'm being so sassy with this complete stranger, who I find wildly attractive. I guess I'm in I've-got-nothing-to-lose mode. He lives in New Mexico, he's too old for me, and I'm never going to see him again.

"Well, since you brought up the position of my rear end, why don't we discuss yours?"

"Excuse me?"

"Take it easy, cowgirl. I'm just wondering what a girl from New Jersey is doing on a horse, in New Mexico, in the middle of summer. Could you have picked a hotter day for a ride?"

I decide to drop the attitude, at least for the moment, and fill him in about how Logan is on his way to ASU, how he'd wanted to bring his car, and the guys decided it would be fun to have a road trip, blah, blah, blah.

"We're leaving him in Tempe with the car and flying home in three days," I explain. Wow. I get a pang when

I realize how soon that is. Not to mention, it's almost the Fourth of July. The thought of it makes me feel hollow inside. Partly because I'm still worried about what I may have said to Joey and partly because I'll be missing the fireworks at home. I've never missed the fireworks at Memorial Field before.

"So, I'm guessing one of the three amigos is your boyfriend?" Is he flirting?

"Nope."

Lucca raises his eyebrows. He is flirting. I'm aware that Logan is listening. Matty and Spencer are falling behind, lost in their inane chatter. "So you just decided to go along for the ride?"

"More like was forced to. My parents wanted to keep me away from a guy."

"Ahh."

"My ex. He sort of filed a restraining order against me."

Lucca laughs at that one, but not in a mean way. More like the kind of genuine outburst that occurs when you're caught off guard. His laughter is contagious, and I start giggling too at this crazy girl named Rosie who did this absurd thing back in New Jersey. The ludicrousness of the whole thing becomes clearer with every mile of this road trip.

"Why do I suddenly feel like I should be on my best behavior?" Lucca says.

I shrug. "Part of my charm."

He slows his horse down so that it's next to mine and leans toward me. "So, this is your getaway, then? Welcome to the wild west." He puts out his right hand and reaches for my left for a kind of sideways shake. I'm sort of nervous about taking one hand off the reins, but for Lucca, I do. His calloused hand is strong, manlier than I'm used to. I start imagining what it would be like to feel that hand against my cheek, on my shoulder, around my waist. I gotta stop. I'm getting tingly all over. I guess being on horseback can do that to a girl.

So here I am, almost holding hands with a cowboy on horseback—mountains looming in the distance, the rugged landscape surrounding us—this could be the most romantic thing to happen to me in, well, again, ever. And it would be, if it weren't for the three pairs of eyes I can feel behind me. Maybe I can pretend the three amigos, as Lucca called them, aren't there.

"Is Rosie holding hands with the cowboy?" Spencer shouts.

The blood rushes to my cheeks and even more sweat trickles down the back of my neck.

"What? This darn horse won't move," yells Matty, who has fallen way behind. "What about Rosie and the cowboy?"

I turn around just as a frustrated Matty gives his horse a swift kick with the stirrups. I wince. What is he thinking? He musta put too much somethin'-somethin' in that giddyap because suddenly his horse bolts past Spencer and Logan, picking up steam as he gallops past me and Lucca and down the winding rocky trail before disappearing into the trees. All I hear is the clop, clop, clop of hooves and Matty screaming, "Whoa, horsey, Whoaaaaa!!!"

"Pull back gently on the reins!" Lucca yells. He turns to me, Logan, and Spencer. "Just keep following this trail. The horses know the way. I got this."

Lucca gives his horse a kick, with the correct amount of oomph, and takes off after Matty like a cowboy in a western movie, yelling directions to Matty as he disappears down the trail in a cloud of dust. Hi ho, Lucca; I can watch that guy all day. This is better than *True Grit*.

"There goes your hero," Logan says as his horse walks beside mine. He gazes off down the trail without looking at me. "Did Matty really yell 'horsey'?"

"Poor bastard. I hope he's okay," Spencer says, then asks, "Why were you holding the cowboy's hand anyway, Rosie?"

"Lucca. His name is Lucca, not the cowboy. And I wasn't holding his hand; I was shaking it."

"I thought we got the introductions over with before we started the ride," Logan says.

I scrunch my eyes at him without saying a word. Our eyes lock for a few seconds and then he pulls ahead of me on the trail. He rides pretty well.

"Come on, Rosie," Spencer says. "Let's see if we can catch up to Matty."

Spencer is pretty good with his horse too. He guides his horse around me and gets it to canter down the path. Penny must think this seems like a good idea because she does the same. Once she gets going, it's bumpier than I expected. My butt keeps smacking against the saddle as she picks up speed. Poor gal. I wonder if having a first-timer on her back is uncomfortable for her. She's probably about ready to drop me at the car and return to her shady barn, but I'm not ready for this ride to end.

When we catch up to them, Lucca is standing in the trail, holding two sets of reins as he tightens the saddle on

Matty's horse. Matty is sitting on a big gray rock, wiping blood off of his forehead.

"Oh my God, Matty! Are you okay?" I want to get off Penny and run to him, but I'm not exactly sure how to go about accomplishing this. I feel trapped.

"I'm fine. It's just a scratch."

"His horse took him under a branch and sort of scraped him off," Lucca says.

"Dude, you were thrown from your horse? How cool," Spencer says.

"I wouldn't say thrown. It was more of a slow slide." Matty sounds dejected.

Lucca nods in agreement and, to his credit, tries to make Matty feel better. "It's good to fall every once in a while. It means you're learning something. He got right up too. I was impressed."

Lucca finishes adjusting the saddle, and a red-cheeked Matty gets in position to mount up. Like a parent watching her kid take his first swing at Little League, my muscles tighten in anticipation. It only takes him one try to get on the horse this time.

"How 'bout you ride up here with me?" Lucca suggests to Matty. Business before romance, I guess. He doesn't need Matty breaking a bone and suing his father.

Now that I'm a horse away from Lucca, I'm not able to talk to him. In a way, it's better. I'm able to focus on the ride. I'm horseback riding in the Sandia Mountains. When will I be able to say that again? I watch the twitch of Penny's ears, inhale through my nose, and exhale slowly through my mouth. Everything else feels so far away, and I'm surprised to find I'm not thinking about anything, or anyone, as I enjoy the sound of horse hooves clopping along the trail. My hearts sinks as we descend the mountain and I see the ranch in the distance.

When we reach the ranch, we gather in front of the barn, where Lucca and his dad supervise our collective dismounts. Lucca holds Penny's reins and puts a hand in the small of my back as I swing my right leg over my horse and lower it to the ground. I take my left foot out of the stirrup and look up at him. I have the sudden urge to touch the charm around his neck.

"Is this the sun?" I ask, taking the medallion in my hand.

"A glyph."

"Huh?" I'm still holding it in my hand.

"Native American sun symbol. Like hieroglyphics."

"Was it made by Native Americans?" Now that we're

not on horseback anymore, I notice he's not that tall—but his chiseled features more than make up for his average height.

"Nah. Some band I saw in Arizona. Bought it off their merch table."

I had almost forgotten my question. *Do not stare directly at Lucca,* I caution myself.

"Nice." I let go of the charm, keeping my eyes fixed on it as I do.

"How long are you in New Mexico for?"

"We're leaving for Arizona from here." Lucca's dark brown eyes search for mine, but I have to look away. Now is not the time to form new attachments.

"Next time you visit, try to do it in the fall. The weather is better, and every October, Albuquerque has its International Balloon Fiesta. Ever been in a hot air balloon?"

"No. But I'd never been on a horse until today either."

"And look how well that turned out. If you decide to do it, look me up. I'll take you for a ride. You'll love floating with the clouds."

My stomach already feels like it is. I know Lucca is just being friendly, but my resistance is fading. Could I make it to Albuquerque in the fall? I'm afraid to look at the guys. I sense they're the ones doing the eye rolling now.

"Call me here when you need to plan your next get-away." Then Lucca leans in and gives me an innocent, but sweet, kiss on my cheek. His scruff gives me chills.

I turn to see Lucca's dad and my three guys staring at us. We stare back at them. It's like a gun duel at the OK Corral. Matty is the first to make a move. He runs a finger along the scrape on his forehead. Logan turns and walks toward the car. Lucca's dad tells him to bring the horses into the barn. Lucca starts to lead Penny away from me, then stops. He takes off his necklace and walks back. In one quick motion, he fastens it around my neck.

"I can't take this," I say.

"How 'bout you give it back next time I see you. You know where to find me." He gives me a crooked, flirty smile, then saunters back to Penny. I think we both know we're never going to see each other again, but I like the idea of having a cowboy in New Mexico to fantasize about whenever I'm in a funk.

Matty waits for me. He puts an arm on my shoulder, buddylike, and leads me toward the car.

"It always starts off well, doesn't it? Let's go before Lucca's horse ends up like Joey's Mustang."

I shrug off his hand and shoot him a cold, hard stare. Matty smiles and throws his arms up in surrender. "Just trying to be helpful."

I give him my give-me-a-break face as he opens the door for me. I'm not really mad; I know he's only joking. As Matty walks around the car to his side, I stand there for a few seconds, my hand on the door, gazing at the barn and the mountains beyond. It's funny, I think as I slip inside and slam the car door shut. It's Penny, not Lucca, who I'm already missing.

Chapter 15

The ride from New Mexico to Arizona is the most tedious stretch of the journey thus far. Outside the car, the scenery is flat, brown, and repetitive, while inside, it is ridiculously—no, make that annoyingly—silent. Here we go again. At least girls have actual hormonal shifts that account for their mood swings. It's biology. But these three, what's their excuse?

For the first hour, Logan won't turn on the car stereo. Matty has his earbuds in, Spencer is fingering the strings of his guitar without strumming, and I'm listening to my own tunes. Even though I've got control of my phone (Matty handed it to me when we got in the car), I'm having trouble getting cell reception out here. I keep waiting for someone to say something—anything. I see signs for Historic

Route 66, but no one even mentions it. I remember this section of Spencer's itinerary. He called it "The Mother Road."

I'm shocked and disappointed when I yell, "Hey, look, we're coming up to the Continental Divide!" and no one acknowledges that I've spoken. I'm not even sure what it is, just seems like something this crew would be interested in. Why are they mad at me? It's not like I was making out with Lucca. And I'm not the one who kissed him on the cheek. Or gave him Native American jewelry. Fine. If they want to play the silent treatment game, I'm going to win. Honestly, it's like they don't want me to be happy. One step up, two steps back. I am so freakin' sick of this car and them.

I turn up the volume on my music, fold my arms, close my eyes, and plan to sleep until we reach the Grand Canyon. I can't believe I felt wistful about leaving the ranch and this trip coming to an end. I want to see my family and my girlfriends. I want to sleep in my own bed. I want to get my stupid effin' court date over with and get on with my summer routine. This sucks! I am throwing a mental tantrum. I am done with these three. I wonder if I can ignore them for the rest of the trip. It's been days since Dollywood, and I'm ready for this roller-coaster ride to be done.

✳   ✳   ✳

About thirty minutes later, Matty points a pack of spearmint gum my way. "Want some?" he asks. I pretend to sleep. A few minutes after that, Spencer says, "We're almost to Gallup." I ignore him, too. It's always on their terms. Well, I hope they're catching a breeze right now.

"We'll be stopping for food and gas when we get there," Logan says. "If she wants to sleep, or pretend to sleep, let her."

What I want to do is kick him in the back of the head with my foot, but I keep up my game of possum. Besides, I can eat without talking. A minute later, the car slows to a stop and Logan puts it in park. That was fast. But when Logan starts pounding the steering wheel and yelling, "Shit, shit, shit," I open my eyes and see that we're on the side of the road, not in the parking lot of some fast-food restaurant.

"Flat?" Matty asks.

Spencer leans over to look at the gauges. "Outta gas," he sighs.

This is so not Logan. His personality is definitely lacking in some areas, but I've always felt safe with him. He's like my dad: always in control, always knowing things, like when we're running low on fuel and where we're supposed to be and when. I'm feeling a little sorry for him but quickly push it away.

"Matty and I will walk down the interstate and get

some gas. It's only a few miles," Logan says. I look down the road. I can see the next exit from here. It doesn't look that far, but nothing does on the open road. Who knows how long it will take them. And it's disgustingly hot outside. "Spence, you and Rosie stay here with the car."

I pull out a bottle of water from my backpack and hand it to Matty. "Take this. And buy yourself some more at the gas station before you walk back. You need to stay hydrated."

"Thanks, Rosie." He looks less than thrilled to have been enlisted to make the long, sweltering trek with Logan the Grouch.

I watch them walk along the shoulder until their shapes blur in the heat rising off the pavement. Then I join Spencer, who is sitting on the trunk strumming his guitar. He plays a classic rock riff I recognize from Guitar Hero and segues into another song.

"This is my Monsters of Rock Guitar medley."

"You're really good," I say. "How about playing me something I know."

Without even thinking about it, he launches into the chorus of "Rosalita."

"Am I that predictable? A New Jersey girl who likes Bruce?"

"Predictable?" He shakes his head and chuckles. "No."

"Can't deny my love for Bruce."

"Nothing wrong with that. He's a genius. Anyway, I know you're named after the song."

"Matty," I say.

"Talks about you all the time. You know—"

I hold up my hand. I'm feeling embarrassed, for me and Matty. Spencer is about to tell me something that, on some level, I've always known. "I don't think I should hear this."

"Got it. No words. Does that apply to my brother, too? You do know why he's acting this way, right?"

What about Avery? I want to say. But really, I don't want to delve into Logan's or Matty's or even Avery's psyche. I've already made a mess of my love life. No need to enter into a love rhombus. Instead, I take the guitar from Spencer. "Do you think you can teach me to play this thing?"

"For real?"

"Yes, for real. I want you to show me what you showed Matty. I want to be able to play a song."

"Okay, then. Let's start with a G chord."

Spencer puts the guitar on my lap. He takes my left hand and places it on the guitar's neck and drapes my right hand on the body. Then he carefully manipulates my pinkie, middle, and pointer fingers into the correct positions on the nylon strings.

"Push down on these three strings. Careful not to touch the others."

I push down as hard as I can. It's not easy to hold them down, though.

"Good," Spencer tells me. "Now, take your thumb like this—" He grabs my right hand. "And strum." He guides my hand across all five strings.

"That sounded like crap," I say.

"It did. Playing guitar is harder than it looks."

"I can't keep the string down and strum at the same time. This is very uncomfortable."

"I hate to say this. . . ." Spencer trails off.

"What? You don't think you can teach me?"

"You may not want to learn when you hear this: The fingernails must go."

"What?"

"You must suffer for art."

I look down at my hands and the pretty gel manicure I got with Avery. My nails aren't super long and I don't wear acrylic tips or anything, but still. I like the length and how they look with polish. Do I want to sacrifice my happy hands?

I let out a deep breath. "I don't have a nail clipper."

Spencer pulls his keys from his pocket. Of course, he's got one dangling from the ring. Right next to a pocketknife.

"Hand it over," I say. I clip all ten nails extra short and dust the shavings onto the ground.

"I'm proud of you," Spencer says. His face looks so sweet when he smiles. "Ready to try the G again?"

"I'm all yours."

I struggle but keep strumming. Spencer coaches me. "Nice and even. That's it." And then on about my fifteenth try, it sounds like something.

"There's your G!" He's all excited. "Now keep going. Once you master that, I'll teach you the D."

My left hand is getting sweaty, so I wipe it on my shirt and then realize I've forgotten where I'm supposed to put my fingers. Spencer takes my fingers and gently places them where they belong.

"What's it feel like?" Spencer asks.

"Guitar strings?"

"No, being in love. Is it worth it?"

It's an interesting time to ask this. I'm sitting on the trunk of a Taurus, guitar in my hand, taking lessons from a guy who, six days ago, was a complete stranger to me, and why? Joey. Still, I do my best to sift through the bad stuff in my brain and find those golden moments—the ones I hope to feel again someday.

The right corner of my mouth turns up as I remember the rush and excitement of falling in love with Joey. Those first days, weeks, months, were amazing. I thought about him all the time. I had no appetite and dropped seven pounds without dieting. I hardly slept but was never tired and woke up before my alarm most mornings. I couldn't wait to start a new day even though Joey and I didn't go to the same school. That part was hard. We couldn't see each other between classes or at lunch, but every text and phone call gave me a rush. Going to different schools heightened the thrill of seeing his car in my school's parking lot after the dismissal bell. And no matter how often I saw him, it never felt like enough. Back then, I never could've imagined hating him. I never wanted to let him go. I certainly couldn't have predicted the events that led me to this moment in New Mexico.

Spencer, who has been waiting for an answer, misreads my silence. "I'm sorry. I probably shouldn't have brought that up."

"No, it's fine. At first, it was the greatest feeling in the world. The anticipation of seeing him. The buildup to our first date, our first kiss. But then—"

Do I tell him what's it's like when that's over and heartbreak settles into the place where all those good feelings used to live? How the days seemed so, so long and I couldn't sleep at night but I didn't want to get out of bed because nothing felt as good as when I was with Joey? TV, magazines, even talking to my friends, all seemed tedious. I was uptight and distracted. All I had focused on for the past nine months was Joey, and I wasn't sure what to do once he was gone.

But I don't tell Spencer any of that. He'll have to find out for himself. Not that I wish it on him; I don't. But we all have to go through it at least once, don't we? Instead, I just look at Spencer and say: "Well, you know what happened. Here I am, right?"

"It hasn't been so bad, has it?"

I look at Spencer and wonder if he's ever been kissed. "Can I ask you something?"

"I guess," Spencer says.

"Have you ever—" I stop. I don't want to embarrass him. Not Spencer.

"What?" He nudges me.

I reach for his hair and comb my fingers through his

super-straight bangs so they look more tousled and less like his mom cuts his hair. "I was just gonna ask you if you've ever thought of using some product. Here, let me get some gel."

Spencer surprises me and moves his hand up to meet mine. "No, you weren't."

And then I shock myself. I slide my fingers to his cheeks and then, without thinking, I lean my face close, which isn't easy with this guitar in my lap, and kiss him on the lips.

Impulsive. It should be my legal middle name.

I pull back for a second. He's one of the good guys and deserves it. Not that I'm saying he deserves me, but he deserves to be kissed.

And while I'm mulling over all this, Spencer catches me off guard and kisses me back. A real kiss this time. It's soft and sweet and makes me wish I could fall for Spencer, but I can't. When it's over, I realize I'm holding my breath and my knees are shaking. The boy's got some skills.

"You're really good at that," I say.

"*Cosmo*. Great for research." Spencer smiles.

"I'm sorry," I say. "I probably shouldn't have done that. I can't explain why I do anything lately and—"

"Don't take this the wrong way. I'm thrilled to have that first kiss out of the way, and it's not that you aren't pretty, because you are. You totally are. But I can't say I exactly . . ."

"Felt anything?" I offer.

"You either, huh?"

Relief. It passes over both our faces. I can tell.

"Yeah, but that's okay. Save that research for a girl you're really crushing on."

Despite the fact that we're both cool with what transpired, I bite my lip and worry about what I've just done.

"Rosie, relax. He doesn't have to know about this."

"Who?"

He shrugs.

"I don't know what you mean. It doesn't have to be a secret or anything."

But Spencer knows that I know he's got me all figured out. It's nice that I've pretty much exorcised Joey from my heart, but it's getting crowded in there. I think I need to reserve some space near my aorta or something. The last thing I want is to arrive back in New Jersey more confused than when I left. Spencer points to the guitar.

"Back to work," he says. "Two more chords and you'll be able to play 'Free Falling.'"

And then he starts singing about a good girl who loves horses.

I don't know why, maybe it's the sweet sound of Spencer's voice, but my eyes brim with tears.

Spencer stops. "Rosie? Are you okay?"

"Can you teach me something edgier? Maybe something by Pink? 'Free Falling' is too sad." The way Spencer looks at me makes the words pour out. "I used to think I was a good girl. But the truth is, I did a bad thing. I keep trying to justify it by blaming Joey for being a cheating asshole, but he didn't make me feel this bad. I did this. I'm humiliated, mortified, disappointed, and disgusted with myself. I mean, he cheated on me, right? So that's a pretty good indication that he didn't love me anymore. Maybe he never loved me. And what did I do? I could have played it cool. Let him have his jailbait and kept my dignity. But I practically announced to the whole world how badly he hurt me. How much I still loved him. Why did I do that, Spencer, why?"

I jump off the trunk and stand there on the side of the highway and throw my arms in the air in a giant V, the guitar still hanging around my neck. "I shouldn't have lost control," I wail. "And now Joey's telling lies about me, saying I did things with him that I've never done with anyone. Look at where being Rosie has gotten me."

Spencer blinks. "I hope I'm so in love with a girl some-day that her breaking up with me would make me want to blow up her car. Well, that sounded bad, but you know what I'm saying. It just means whatever you do, whoever you care about, you're in it all the way. And that's nothing to feel bad, or humiliated, about."

"You really think so?"

"Yes. I do. I think you just need an outlet for all that . . . passion."

"I am passionate, aren't I? That's what I tried to tell Matty."

"And for the record, Joey cheated on you because he found a girl who would do what you wouldn't."

"I'm not so sure." All this time, I figured it was because there's something wrong with me.

"I am. I go to school with him, not that he would know that. I've seen him in action. If Joey wanted a girlfriend, he never would have broken up with you. So don't be surprised."

"About what?"

"If he wants you back."

"I'm tired of surprises. Lately, things aren't turning out the way I planned."

"Good or bad, nothing ever does," Spencer says.

"Fortune cookie?"

"Nah." He shakes his head. "All me."

Logan and Matty finally return, gas can and water bottles in hand. They're both bright red and sweaty. Logan promptly fills the tank and Matty raises his eyebrows at the guitar. If this surprises him, he should have been here twenty minutes ago. That would have given him an eyeball full.

"Spencer's going to teach me to play 'Free Falling,'" I blurt out.

"Glad you used this time to pursue your latent artistic urges," Matty says.

"Spencer thinks I need to channel my passion," I reply.

"How about you start by driving," Logan says. He tightens the gas cap and walks around to the back of the car to face me.

"He speaks," I say.

"I speak," he says.

Logan lets his hand linger in mine as he gives me the keys, and I wish his touch didn't make every last inch of me want to kiss him, sweaty and all. No more boys. Guitar. I'm going to learn guitar. He looks more relaxed than when he left, and I hate to admit, but I'm relieved he's not ignoring me anymore.

"Feel like driving us to the gas station?"

"Sure." I lift the guitar strap off my shoulder and hand the acoustic to Spencer. "Let's go. I'm starving."

"You're starving?" Matty says. "I just sweat off my last three meals."

Logan pats him on the back. "Thanks for coming, man. Why don't you take shotgun until we get to Arizona?"

Matty eyes him suspiciously. I can't say that I blame him. What happened during that walk to make Logan so nice?

Heatstroke. That must be it. Logan has heatstroke.

Chapter 16

My phone rings when we're en route to the Grand Canyon. I'm driving and have been since we stopped for gas in New Mexico. Matty checks the caller ID. "Lilliana."

"Hold it up to my ear," I say. Matty doesn't move. "Please. Can you please hold the phone up to my ear?"

"Why, yes I can," Matty says. "'Please' and 'thank you' are the magic words."

Lilliana doesn't even wait for me to say hello. "How does Joey know you're going to be in Phoenix on the Fourth of July?" she demands.

I'm so shocked, I forget to censor what I'm saying. "How do you know that Joey knows I'm going to be in Phoenix on the Fourth of July?" It's a good thing I'm driving so I can't see Matty's face, especially since I never answered him when he asked almost the exact same thing in Texas. At the time, I thought it was possible Joey could have found out about my trip from someone else, but Phoenix on the Fourth, that's all me.

"He sent me a message on Facebook last night," she screeches. "He told me you sent him a message on Facebook a week ago, telling him to meet you there. He wanted to know if I thought you were serious. So are you? Serious? Why would you tell him that? Would have been nice of you to tell your best friend that you told your ex-boyfriend to meet you in Arizona."

Ah. Facebook. I'm not usually one for social media. I don't update my status with cryptic messages every twenty minutes. I hardly ever sign on. But that explains it. I don't remember booting up my laptop during my antihistamine haze, but there ya go. Another brilliant move by Rosalita Ariana Catalano. Not to mention another TRO violation. Why didn't I mention it to anybody? Because I was hoping that after all my mortifying and desperate acts in the last few weeks, that one wasn't real. I was doing the guy thing. Ignoring it and hoping it would just go away.

"What did you tell him?" I ask.

"I wanted to talk to you first," Lilliana says. She sounds

angry or maybe just annoyed. Either way, it's disconcerting coming from her.

"Why do you think he wants to know if I'm serious?"

Lilliana hesitates, then exhales loudly, clearly exasperated by Joey. Or me. Both, probably. "No clue. Do you think he wants you back?"

At first my heart does a triple salchow at the sound of those words. It would be a small victory of sorts, but the ho and TRO are hard to get past. The person he turned me into that night . . . that's even harder. I don't want to be her anymore. In the past few days, I've come a long way and, well, I've come a long way. Right?

"He's up to something," I conclude.

"Do you think he'll go to Phoenix?"

"I don't know."

"You don't know?! You don't seriously want him back, do you?"

"I need to think."

"What is there to think about? Let me tell him to go eff himself. I can say the Fourth of July message didn't come from you. That someone hacked into your account."

"I'll call you back."

"Whatever. Take your time." Then Lilliana hangs up

on me. I don't blame her. I'm fed up with me too.

I know Lilliana is right. But what if Joey contacted her because he does want me back? I think about what Spencer said. It's possible, right? That it could be the answer to all my problems. He could drop the TRO and we could get back together. True, what I'm feeling for him now is close to hate, but I could suck it up, date him for a month, and show him what it's like to be the dumpee. I'd get closure sans a criminal record, squash any rumors about me, and finish out high school without some horrible nickname. What's not to like about that plan?

My mind starts reeling. Do I call my parents and Steve Justice to come clean about the Facebook message to Joey? Do I call Lilliana back and tell her to tell Joey to eff himself? I know she'll be disappointed if I don't. What am I doing? How can I even consider taking him back? What then? We rendezvous in Phoenix and fly home together as a happy couple? Ugh. I hate this! I have this sudden urge to talk to Avery.

"Are you okay there, Rosie?" Spencer is leaning between the front seats.

"Fine. Why?"

"Because you're doing a hundred and one in a seventy-five-mile-per-hour zone," Matty offers.

Yikes! He's right. It's hard to tell out here. A person can drive for miles without seeing another car. "Can we switch drivers soon? I've got some calls I need to make."

"We're stopping in Williams," Logan says. "We'll switch then. In the meantime, ease back off the gas, pardner."

"I gotta say. Traveling with Rosie is like overhearing my mom's soap opera in the next room," Spencer says.

"Overhearing? Who are you kidding?" Matty says. "I've watched *General Hospital* with you on SOAPnet. It's addicting."

"Anything I can do, Rosalita?" Logan asks empathetically.

I make a quick mental list. Kick Joey's ass. Tell Joey off. Take Joey's place. I recognize that last one is not the answer to all my problems. Most likely just the beginning of new ones. Or maybe not. Logan is not Joey.

"I'm good," I say, and keep my eyes straight ahead and don't say another word until I see our exit and pull into the small town that is our destination.

WELCOME TO WILLIAMS, ARIZONA! GATEWAY TO THE GRAND CANYON; that's what the sign said when we arrived fifteen minutes ago.

"More like gateway to the weird," I mumble. I'm not trying to be judgmental, but I'm standing next to a fifty-foot-tall Fred Flintstone, my arm reaching upward as I pretend to hold his hand while Matty and Spencer take my picture. We're at the Yabba-Dabba-Doo campsite and theme park. Ha! Theme park. For five bucks visitors can walk around the village of Bedrock, where Fred and his buddies lived. This place is as old as the original cartoon. There's a giant dinosaur slide, which looks somewhat tempting, but when I get to the top, it smells like pee and there's no way in hell my tush is touching that thing. I urge the boys to retreat back down the dino-tail steps.

We walk around the rest of Williams, which is kind of quaint. There's lots of Route 66 signage and plenty of stores on Main Street that sell memorabilia from the old Mother Road.

"Williams has the distinction of being the last town on Route 66 to be bypassed by the interstate," Spencer reads from a placard outside one of the shops.

"Aw. Just like that Disney movie with cars," I recall.

"*Cars?*" Matty says sarcastically.

"That's it!" I say.

We grab a quick lunch at Subway and then walk around some more. I'm procrastinating. I know I should call Lilliana back.

"I'm going to gas up the car," Logan says. We probably only burned a quarter of a tank, but I guess he's not taking any chances.

"We'll get some supplies at that market over there," Spencer says.

"Okay. Let's meet in front of the store in twenty minutes," Logan says.

While Spencer and Matty wander around inside—I told them to get me a snack—I stay outside and make some calls. Just thinking about the sound of my mom's voice gets me all choked up. I can't quite bring myself to reveal my latest Joey transgression. I decide to start with Miranda. It's probably more important that Steve Justice know about this anyway. But when Miranda answers the phone and finds out it's me, she doesn't give me a chance to come clean.

"I'm glad you called. I've got good news," Miranda says.

"How good? Do you think he might drop the whole thing?"

I mean, if what Lilliana suspects is true and Joey wants me back, it wouldn't be a stretch, would it? He'd be out of his mind to think I'd want to be with him again if the TRO's hanging over our heads.

"Don't get your hopes up about that," Miranda says.

But we found a neighbor who was home the night of the fire and claims she saw everything. I'm going out to speak with her and record her statement tomorrow."

"Wow. That is good news. Will you let me know what she says?"

"Don't worry. We'll talk about everything during your meeting with Steve, before the hearing. Just pu-lease try to stay out of trouble until then," Miranda says.

She makes it sound so easy, I think as I disconnect my phone. I should call Lilliana back, apologize, and urge her to get in touch with Joey immediately to put the brakes on this thing, but I can't, not yet. First, I want to talk to Avery.

"What am I gonna do?" I ask her. "Do you think he wants me back? Would he actually come to Arizona?"

"First, you're going to breathe," Avery tells me. "Then you're going to check your backpack for the care package I slipped in for you. I can't believe you haven't found it yet."

"It's a mess in there," I admit. I've been stuffing things in without bothering to look or clean up the clutter.

"When's your court date?" Avery asks.

"July ninth. Not until Thursday. I lucked out because of the holiday."

"There you go. Whatever's gonna happen won't happen until then. Make the rest of this trip about you, missy. Got it?"

"But what about Joey; what should I do?"

"Do what you gotta do."

"Uh-huh." That's not very specific. I want to press her for a more definitive answer, but I get the feeling she's not going to offer me one. "Hey, so when do you leave to build houses?" I don't want Avery thinking everything always has to be about me.

"Not until August. I'm waiting until it's good and hot so I can suffer." She laughs. "I'm excited. These houses are going to be totally eco-friendly and sustainable." There we go with that word again. "Don't worry," she says before she hangs up. "I know you know what to do." That silly, sweet girl has apparently already forgotten about the brawl I started less than thirty-six hours ago at the club.

Two minutes after I hang up with Avery, Matty and Spencer come out of the store carrying a Styrofoam cooler. I wonder what Logan will say about the non-eco-friendly material.

"What did you guys get?"

"Drinks and snacks and stuff," Matty says offhandedly.

"We're not that far away from the Grand Canyon, are we?" I'm suddenly tired thinking about another three-hour stretch in the car.

"About an hour, but we may get hungry and thirsty while we're there," Spencer says. "The restaurant in the lodge looks pricey."

Logan pulls up and I expect them to fight for shotgun, but they both get into the backseat without a word. Fine by me. I didn't exactly want to ride with a cooler and a guitar.

"Can you pass me my backpack?" I ask after I'm settled into the front seat.

"Sure thing," Matty says, passing it forward. He doesn't ask for my phone, and I don't offer it up. I know I've got to call Lilliana soon. I unzip my backpack. As I root past my makeup bag, dwindling snack supply, random receipts, napkins, magazines, and two copies of the trip itinerary, I see a Ziploc bag with a Post-it note that says *For your reading and listening pleasure. It's all about the possibilities. XOXO Avery.*

Inside are two brochures, one from ASU and the other from Habitat for Humanity, and a USB flash drive on which Avery has written in tiny pink letters AVERY'S BOYS SUCK, GIRLS RULE MIX. I feel like I'm thirteen again.

"Hey, Spence," I say, waving the USB into the backseat.

"Can you help me download these to my iPod the next time we stop?"

No answer.

"Spence?"

When I turn around, Matty and Spencer are shielding their faces behind the Styrofoam cooler lid.

"Are you two sneaking food?" I say. "What's the big deal? Oh my God, you aren't kissing, are you?" This elicits groans of disgust all around.

"They're sneaking beer," Logan says, like a parent who can't be fooled.

"How'd you know?" Spencer asks.

"Did you think I wasn't gonna hear you pop the bottle caps?"

"You got served?" I'm shocked. They both look twelve.

"They were selling beer next to the soda," Matty says. "We just put it on the counter with the other stuff and the kid behind the register never said a word."

"You're okay with this?" I look at Logan.

He shrugs. "As long as they're not driving. And don't get caught." I can tell he's not really cool with it, but he's trying to be.

As we get closer and closer to the entrance to Grand

Canyon National Park, the laughter in the backseat gets louder and louder. I'm reading through both of Avery's brochures and learning some interesting facts about both ASU and Habitat for Humanity. I make two very important discoveries.

1. ASU does not allow freshmen to have cars on campus.
2. Jimmy Carter and his wife, Rosalynn, made the first Habitat trip in 1984 and raised the visibility of the organization tremendously.

I was too embarrassed at the time to ask Avery what Jimmy Carter had to do with her inspiration to build houses this summer. I can't wait to listen to Avery's mix to see what other startling revelations I can make. I take out my phone and think about calling Lilliana just as Matty lets out a loud burp.

"I hope they've got railings at the Grand Canyon," I say.

"Not many. We'll keep an eye on them," Logan says. Logan turns to look into the backseat. "We're almost to the entrance, you two. How 'bout you put away those open containers and close the cooler?"

We pay the admission fee at the toll booth and get a

map of the various lookout points we can drive to by car, as well as the hiking trails and information about mule and helicopter rides—neither of which I'm interested in. We drive for a few miles before I catch my first glimpse of the canyon near the Desert View observation point.

"Holy Mother of God!" I yell. "Pull the car over!"

Matty lets out another loud burp. "Jeez, Rosie. What is it? Another McDonald's shaped like a flying saucer?"

We clamber out of the car, and it may sound like an exaggeration, but the view literally takes my breath away. The Grand Canyon is its own kind of wonderful. The sheer vastness, the shadows and changing colors, the depth and stillness. I never thought anything except the ocean could silence my thoughts and make me feel so free.

Moments later, a small mishap occurs while Spencer is taking a picture of drunk Matty and me. Matty's in that "I love you, man" kind of mood and wants one of just the two of us for, as he puts it, *Matty's Memoirs*. Our backs are against the lookout railing, and I prop my foot on the lower rung. The vastness of the Grand Canyon stretches behind us. It's so perfect, it almost looks like a photographer's backdrop.

"This one will be a keeper," Matty says, and we put an arm around each other.

Just after Spencer snaps the picture, my foot slides off the railing and I accidentally kick myself in the butt (probably long overdue), which sends my phone flying out of my jean shorts and over the edge. It falls about twenty feet before smashing to pieces on the rocks. It's like the umbilical cord that's been stretching since I left New Jersey finally snaps. Matty and I peer over the railing. My first thought is, I hope I don't get some kind of littering violation. Other than that, I've got nothing.

"Well, as much as that sucks," Matty says, "I am thrilled to be free of your mom's constant barrage of communiqués. I am *so* tired of my pockets vibrating."

Just then, Matty makes a strange face.

"Your pants are vibrating, aren't they?"

"It's her," Matty says, looking at his cell. "I bet she thinks you're dead. Here, you take it." He hands me the phone like it's a bomb.

I put my hands up. "Oh, no, Mr. Rosie Needs to Get Out of Dodge. This one is all you. And don't let her know you're shit faced."

Matty answers. I hear screaming on the other end. "No, Mrs. Catalano, we're fine. Rosie didn't fall into the Grand Canyon. I know. I know. That's some GPS you had on that phone. Yes, I said 'had.' Uh, here, talk to Rosie."

This time, Matty tosses me the phone like it's on fire. "Hi, Ma. I'm fine. No, no, it wasn't the satellites, either. It was my phone. It fell out of my pocket. That's why you lost the signal." I hold the speaker away from my ear so I don't have to hear her bilingual tirade. Finally, she gives me a chance to speak again. "It's only a couple more days, Ma. We'll just use Matty's phone, but not too much, okay? It's not fair to burn his minutes. Okay, okay. Love you too."

Let's see, Dollywood tickets, a guitar for Matty, and a new phone for me. I'll be working at the lampshade factory, walking dogs, and, ugh, babysitting until Halloween. For some inexplicable reason, I don't care. I feel lighter, like that phone was weighing me down. I'm glad I cut it loose. I'm happy I can't be "watched" anymore. I inhale deeply through my nose. Priceless.

"Hey, have you guys even checked in with your parents once?" I ask the boys. "Why am I the only one with parents who chart my every movement?"

"I told them I'd let them know when we got there," Logan says.

"My mom has a no-news-is-good-news policy. And

anyway, she's knows your mom is manning command central next door," Matty replies.

"Hey, don't diss my mom," I warn.

We explore the South Rim for the rest of the afternoon, stopping at various lookout points, before ending up at a spot near the lodge, where we plan to stay until sunset. Spencer is dying to take some more pictures. He and Matty want to hike down a ways into the canyon, and I'm nervous about letting them go too far, but Logan thinks they're both sober again. I find a spot without a railing and dangle my feet over the edge and recline with my arms spread out behind me. Logan sits next to me and assumes a similar position. We watch as Spencer and Matty make their way along a narrow trail below us. Every now and then one of them looks up and waves. At one point, Matty snaps a picture of me and Logan, then he signals their destination ahead: a large white rock that will require them jumping over a two-foot crevice. I'm not going to relax until they make it there safely.

"It's such a long way down," I say.

"A mile." Logan sits up and points down into the canyon. "Do you know at the very base of the canyon, along the river, the rock exposed in that lowest stratum is two thousand million years old?"

"You're making that number up."

"I am not."

"Isn't one thousand million a billion? Can't you just say two billion?"

"Fine. So, the Precambrian rocks at the bottom are two billion years old. The strata near the top are only 250 million years old and from the Paleozoic era."

"It's good to know that when your brother gets trashed, you're here to pick up the factoid slack."

For that, I get a full smile complete with dimple. It's like Logan glows from inside when he drops his guard. When he leans back again, his hand is closer to mine and I can feel the energy between our fingertips.

I try to focus on Logan's paleontology lesson. It's not easy. It doesn't help that I have zero interest in rocks, no matter how pretty they are. "So the deeper you go, it's like going back in time?" I ask.

"Sort of. Exposed rocks closer to three billion years old have been found in Africa, Australia, and the Canadian Shield."

I reply with my own little factoid. "Do you know that

ASU does not allow freshmen to have cars on campus?"

Logan doesn't say anything. He just nods.

"So, this whole road trip wasn't about wanting your car out here, was it?"

"It was and it wasn't. I wanted to give Spencer some time away from our town. Our house. Our—"

"Father?"

"Especially him."

"Are things that bad at home?"

Logan sighs. "I can't speak for my mom and Spencer, but things between me and my dad . . . let's just say, I seem to be the target of his anger when he's drunk. But now, well, I'm done."

Logan always seems so in control. Older than the rest of us. But as he talks about his father, it's like I can see Logan as a kid, the bruised little boy who never quite healed.

"I'm so sorry."

"Why? It's not your fault my father's a bastard. I think it will be better for everyone now that I'll be away at college."

Logan clenches his jaw. His cheeks flush with anger. "And if things ever get unbearable for my brother, he can always come out to Arizona and stay with me."

"If I had known . . . I shouldn't have horned in on your

time with your brother. I get it now, you know, why you were so mean to me in the beginning."

"Are you kidding? Spencer loves having you around. You make a much better first kiss than Matty."

My face turns the color of the setting sun. "He told you?"

"Blood is thicker than saliva."

"Ew." I bump shoulders with him. "But what about you? You didn't want me around."

He faces me now. "It wasn't that. It's just . . . I spent my entire senior year focused on one thing—getting to Arizona. Part of that preparation meant making no unnecessary attachments. I didn't even go to my prom. And then you stepped out onto the porch that morning and . . ."

I'm flattered and sad all at the same time. "You're not coming back at all, are you?"

Logan doesn't answer me. He stares straight ahead again. I inch toward him until our thighs and shoulders meet. He slides his hand over until our fingertips touch. I don't know how long we stay that way, but we watch the sun go down together. The giant, burnt-orange sphere sinks toward the horizon, coloring the rock layers until it's gone and the canyon is covered in shadow.

When the boys rejoin us, it's time to leave. It's like I'm

five years old and leaving Disney World. I don't want to go. I wish I could watch the sun set with Logan again and again. I'd never get tired of it.

We leave the Grand Canyon at twilight. It's quiet in the car, in a good way for once. No words, no music. Silence seems right. I roll down the window and lean my head against the door frame, listening to the wind rush by and smelling the pine trees. I watch the stars materialize, like someone is dimming the switch on the night sky so each shining dot grows brighter and brighter.

Logan is the first one to speak. "Change of plans for the night, Catalano. You can have your own space if you want it."

I'm not sure I like that idea. Even though sharing a room with these three can be a big pain in the ass, as I've said from the start, I don't do "alone" very well.

"What, where? Not that Yabba-Dabba-Doo place." The itinerary is a crumpled mess, complete with powered cheese stains, at the bottom of my bag. I saw it down there when I retrieved Avery's goody bag. I don't feel like digging it out.

"No. That was a dump," Matty says.

"You'll see," Spencer says.

About thirty minutes later, near the park entrance, we arrive at a very rustic-looking campsite.

"Oh, I do not do the camping thing. Absolutely not."

"Come on, Rosie. We'll rent you your own tent. Think of it, your very own place," Spencer croons. Yeah, like that's going to make me jump all over this idea. "They have coin-operated showers."

"Coin-operated showers? Well, now, why didn't you say that to begin with? And just what am I supposed to sleep in?"

"Sleep naked. You'll be alone," Logan says. I hear him smiling.

"You know what I mean. No one said I was supposed to bring a sleeping bag."

"Would you have listened?" Logan asks.

"Probably not."

"No worries. I packed one for you," Matty says.

Sigh. The euphoria from visiting a natural wonder is seeping out of my body. Is the Grand Canyon a natural wonder? If not, it should be.

An hour later, after one too many jokes about "pitching a tent," our campsite is set up. I told the guys I didn't want to stay in my own tent, so we rented a family-size one. I'm trying hard not to think about how many germs are in this thing or what kinds of insects we might encounter tonight.

"Are there scorpions around here?" I've got my hands on my hips and I'm scanning the ground.

"I don't think we have to worry about scorpions this far north," Spencer tells me.

Is he telling the truth or trying to make me feel better? I bite my lower lip and look longingly at the car. If I sleep with the windows open, it won't be that bad, will it?

"Should we get a fire started?" Matty asks.

"For what? It's hot out," I say. "Just pointing out the obvious."

"We need to cook the hot dogs," Spencer says. "Plus just wait, the temp is going to go down tonight."

"We have hot dogs?" I ask.

"Cooler," Logan says.

"I thought we had beer in the cooler."

"That too. We scored the beer when we bought the hot dogs," Matty explains.

"Wait a second." I point from Spencer to Logan. "You two don't eat beef."

"A hot dog once in a while won't kill us," Spencer says. "I generally have two a year."

A weenie roast if there ever was one. "Did you get marshmallows?" I ask.

Matty grins. "Of course. Hershey bars and graham crackers too."

S'mores! Oh, thank you, God. Thank you for sending me on this road trip with guys who would rather sit round the campfire making s'mores than dine at Hooters. Somewhere between dinner and dessert, I get that nagging feeling, like I've still got homework to do. I know I should call Lilliana, but I don't want to deal with home and Joey right now. I'm having too much fun.

I have to admit, precamping rocks. We stay up super late, talking and eating. The boys finish off the beer; even Logan has one. I have a few sips but don't finish mine. I really don't like the taste, and I don't want to have to pee in the woods. With this fear in mind, I hit the public bathroom to empty my bladder and change into sleeping shorts and a T-shirt. By the time I arrive back at the tent, I'm thinking sleep should be no problem at all, except that now, thanks to Spencer, it is.

"I need to sleep by the door," he says. "I get claustrophobic."

"I don't want to be on an end," I say. Selfishly, I'm thinking I'd like to have at least one body between me and whatever wild animal may attack us while we sleep. Inevitably, I end up between Logan and Matty. Is it too late to request my own tent?

Spencer falls asleep right away, but despite feeling absolutely wiped, the minute I climb into my sleeping bag, it's like I've drunk a half pot of coffee. I turn right, and I'm facing Matty. No good. I flip the other way, and I'm facing Logan's back. Better. Logan's head is pointed toward the tent wall, so I can't see if his eyes are closed. His arm is resting on his side, and I'm mesmerized by the ripples in his muscles. I stay in that position for a long time, motionless.

I don't know how much time has passed when I finally peer behind me to see if Matty's eyes are closed. They are. But is he asleep? Too late. My hand is as impulsive as the rest of me. I take my pointer finger and run it the full length of Logan's arm, starting at his bare shoulder and running it along his biceps, inside his forearm, and then into his open palm. He doesn't make a move, so I think he's asleep until his fingers close on top of mine. My heart pounds in my ears. I wonder if he'll turn to face me. I wonder what it is I think I'm doing. Then Matty pops up.

"It's too hot in here," he declares. "I'm sleeping outside." He picks up his bag, unzips the tent, and leaves, without bothering to seal the flap behind him. Spencer doesn't even stir; he must be totally out of it.

I get up on all fours and lean over to close the door. Matty's shaking out his bag beside what's left of the campfire. When I turn back, Logan is half out of his sleeping bag facing me. He's just wearing his boxers. He must've slipped his shorts off at some point. He takes his hand and cups the left side of my face, slipping it under my hair. Oh, man.

"Rosie," he whispers.

I press my forehead against his and close my eyes. "I . . . Sorry."

I scramble outside the tent in my bare feet and walk over to Matty. He's already zipped up like a sausage in his sleeping bag. It's chillier than I thought it would be. Spencer was right. Isn't he always? I ease myself onto one of the logs by the fire and don't say a word.

Finally, Matty speaks. "Spencer told me."

"About what?"

"The kiss."

"Oh." I don't know what else to say. It was Spencer's secret to tell. I can't exactly be angry with him. Matty's his best friend. My throat feels like it's closing. Matty is my best friend too.

"He says it was no big thing."

I try to ignore that Spencer's first kiss with me was "no big thing." I'll chalk it up to Spencer trying to be cool. "He needed to get it out of the way, I think."

"And what about you? Is there anything else you need to get out of the way? I guess I'm the only guy you're not going to kiss on this trip."

"I didn't kiss Logan," I protest.

"But you want to."

"That's not fair. You wanted to kiss Avery."

"But I didn't."

"And I didn't kiss Logan."

He scowls. "Yet."

My chest flutters with excitement at the thought of going back into the tent and finishing what I started. I wrap my arms around myself and wiggle my toes, which are starting to feel slightly numb. "Matty . . ."

"What?"

"Is that what you want? Do you think we should kiss?"

He doesn't look at me. "Do you?"

I don't say anything.

"Rosie?" He turns sideways, sits up in his sleeping bag, and finally makes eye contact.

"I can't risk ruining everything we have between us," I say quietly.

"What exactly do we have between us, Rosie? Because I don't know anymore."

"How can you say that? You are my best friend, Matty. More than that. You're like my brother. We know everything there is to know about each other. I know you better than Lilliana, even. I know that when you were ten, you were so afraid of zombies that you slept with the light on for six months. You remembered my Strawberry Shortcake lip gloss obsession. I know you got that scar above your eyebrow from hanging upside down off the monkey bars and falling off. You know what I looked like when I had zits and braces. You've heard me belch. You've seen me cry. You came to my rescue when I made a complete and utter mess out of my life. I'm so grateful for that, I could kiss you right now for just being you. For always being so good in general, and for being good to me specifically. But if I did, and if things didn't work out between us, it wouldn't be like losing some stupid boyfriend like Joey. I would be losing family."

Matty looks at me for a few seconds before throwing open his sleeping bag and patting the space next to him. "Come 'ere," he says. "You look cold."

I hesitate, but then my brain does a mental shrug and I slide off the log and scooch into Matty's sleeping bag. It's a tight fit, but he moves over and tries to keep from touching me. I pull the sleeping bag across me but don't zip it. Ah, I can feel my feet again.

Matty is flat on his back, arms across his chest, looking up at the sky. Finally, he turns to face me. I can feel him smiling. "You think of me as part of your family?"

"Not just me. My parents, Eddie—you've got to know how much you mean to them. The only reason they let me take this trip is because you were going to be with me. If something were to happen between us, it would have to be the kind of something that lasts for a really long time, because they wouldn't want to lose you either."

"So you haven't ruled it out? Us?"

I don't know how to answer that, but I don't want to hurt him. "No. I haven't. But you know I'd be a terrible girlfriend. I'm more like an icky older sister."

Matty uncrosses his arms and puts one under my head. Then he leans over and kisses me on the forehead. "You will never be my icky sister. Crazy sister, yes. But icky? Rosie Catalano, you are not icky."

"Neither are you, Matthew Ryan Connelly. Now,

you're not going to try to grab my boob, are you?"

That gets us giggling like we're kids at our first sleepover. I try to talk, but snorting noises come out of my nose and I can't get a word out. I've forgotten what it's like to laugh like this.

Finally, we settle down and stare up at the endless Arizona sky.

"These stars are amazing. It's like watching a 3-D movie. Some of them really do look close enough to touch." I squint, hold out my hand, and pretend I'm doing just that. I wish someone were taking a picture of me and Matty right now. Curled up together in this sleeping bag. Looking at the universe. Come to think of it, I don't need a picture. Somehow I know, for the rest of my life, no matter where I go or who I end up with, I will never forget this moment.

I turn on my side and close my eyes. Matty drapes his other arm over me, but I don't worry about what it means. Within seconds, he's breathing deep, even breaths. He's asleep. And I'm not far behind. Despite being outside, with no protection from the elements or wild animals, I'm not worried about becoming some coyote's next meal. In fact, I fall into the kind of deep, secure sleep I haven't known since I met Joey all those months ago.

Chapter 17

Our drive south from the Grand Canyon is like
something out of a really cool car commercial. We take Dry
Creek Scenic Road into Sedona, passing these amazing,
giant red rocks that rise above the otherwise flat landscape,
dotted with cacti that look like they have thick, waving
arms. An hour later, we arrive at Sliding Rock Canyon, a
place where people picnic and swim. We all wore bathing
suits under our clothes in anticipation of this stop. I changed
into mine after my coin-operated shower at the campsite. I
brought a fistful of change, not knowing what to expect, but
in the end, it wasn't half bad.

I spread out a towel on the rust-colored flat rocks near
the water's edge and lather on some suntan lotion that
smells like a piña colada. I smile to myself as I think of

Lucca and my Cancún fantasy. He was some cowboy.

It doesn't take long before it gets too hot. To avoid getting all sweaty before it's time to get back in the Taurus, I wade into the creek up to my calves to cool my body and take in the canyon around me. Arizona is beautiful, uniquely so. The colors, the cacti, the sky—I think that's one of my favorite parts, the sky, especially at night. But I don't know if a New Jersey girl like me could ever get used to all this desert sand and no ocean.

I'm standing with my arms crossed over my tankini, watching a mom push her toddler around on his SpongeBob tube, when Logan comes up and stands beside me. Neither of us said anything this morning about the tent incident. And neither of us says anything now, but somehow, it's not awkward.

I haven't taken my shorts off yet. I don't plan on swimming, but I'm hoping to get some nice color from the sun reflecting off the water. I can't come all the way to Arizona and return home without a tan—particularly in July! That would be so wrong.

I close my eyes and let the heat warm my entire body. Sedona is hotter than the Grand Canyon. But Spencer says Phoenix is going to be hotter still, which I remember from checking regional average temps when I was packing.

"So," Logan says.

"So," I reply, looking over the top of my sunglasses at him.

"What do you think?"

I choose to assume he's talking about Sliding Rock. "It's beautiful, really. I can see why you fell in love with it here."

"But?"

"But I'm an ocean girl. I like diving under waves and boogie boarding. I like soft, white sand that squishes between my toes."

"You don't think you could get used to all this?"

Why is he asking me that? Is he envisioning a time when I'd have to get used to Arizona? "I didn't say that I couldn't. Anything is possible." I'm starting to believe that.

Logan nods. Then he puts out his hand. "Let's take a walk."

We walk in the water, hand in hand, neither of us bothering to ask why or what it means. When it starts getting deeper, we move to the edge and walk on the rocks. They're so smooth, it's almost like a man-made water park. Then Logan drops my hand. Matty and Spencer are on top of a nearby ledge waiting their turn to dive in. Matty waves to me before making a perfect swan dive in the water, his lean body entering the creek with hardly a splash.

I don't know if years from now something more will ever happen between us, but Matty will always be my Matty, even if he's not destined to be my soul mate. I can't picture my life without him.

I'm so relaxed when we get back in the car. My skin has a nice glow and still smells like suntan lotion. I pull a tank top on over my bathing suit and settle into the backseat. I scrounge around in my bag for a file so I can fix the damage I did cutting my nails for my guitar lesson. Even if my nails are super short now, I still want them to look good. Plus, filing my nails is like meditation—helps me sort things out.

Spencer's driving, and I don't bother asking how long it will take to get to the Phoenix area; we'll get there when we get there. We're spending tonight in a motel near Tempe, where ASU is. Then we'll be there all day tomorrow, the Fourth of July, before spending one last night in Arizona and Matty, Spencer, and I leave on a red-eye. It feels like summer's end, even though it's just getting started. Sigh.

I'm actually looking forward to checking out ASU. I've never been to any college campuses before, not even Montclair State and Seton Hall, which are both under a half hour from my house. From the pictures in the brochure, ASU looks like a cool place to spend four years. The grass is green, the sky is blue, and the students are all sporting shorts, sandals, and lightweight hoodies. Despite having no ocean, the endless summer aspect of Arizona totally adds points in its favor, and I could start fresh as a new and improved Rosie if I came to college here. Only Avery and Logan would know about Joey and the car. But are these good enough reasons to apply? I guess if it makes you happy. But who knows what the next year will bring? I wonder if Logan and Avery will even consider me a friend by then or if memories of this trip will be the only thing we share.

As I round out the nails on my left hand, I work my way through the layers of emotion. My thoughts feel like a ball made out of rubber bands, tight, compact, and overlapping. The trip ending, my court date coming, telling Joey to meet me in Phoenix, not returning Lilliana's call, kissing Spencer, sleeping with Matty, watching the sun set with Logan, losing my phone, losing my mind, losing my heart. What's going to happen when I get back home?

I bite off a hangnail on my ring finger. Avery is right. There's no use looking beyond my court date—whatever's going to happen will happen. That doesn't mean I can't have a plan, though. I've got to stop letting things just "happen" to me.

I'm imagining taking the elastic ball and throwing it into the desert when Matty's phone rings. Poor guy. I know it's for me. He holds up the phone because it's not my mom and he doesn't recognize the number. Unfortunately, I do. The rubber bands in my head all snap simultaneously.

"Joey."

Spencer gasps. Despite my predicament, this makes me smile. "No shit?" he asks.

"No shit," I say. "I can't talk to him, Matty. I promised my mom, and Miranda will kill me. Let it go to voice mail."

Logan sticks his hand out.

"Give it," he says. *I hope Logan talking to Joey doesn't violate my TRO*, I think as Matty hands him the phone.

We listen to Logan's half of the conversation. "Hello? Who's this? Joey. What can I do for you, Joey? Rosie? Now, you of all people should know that talking to you could get her in big trouble. How about you give me the message? Don't worry about who I am. We'll let it remain a mystery for your crack legal team. . . ." Logan covers the phone and talks to us, "This guy is a douche bag." Then he talks back into the phone. "Back at you, man. How about you drop the attitude and just tell me what the frig you want. . . . Tell Rosie you're not going to be in Phoenix on the Fourth of July? What a coincidence; neither is she." There's a pause and I'm not sure what Joey is saying, but then Logan says, "Sorry. Still can't let you talk to her."

"Tell him I'm taking the red-eye home on Sunday. He can contact my attorney after that."

Logan passes along the message, then simply hangs up.

"What an a-hole," Logan says as he tosses the phone back to Matty.

"He wasn't always," I mumble. "That was not the Joey I dated."

"No offense," Spencer says, "but no one seems to know the Joey you dated."

"Word," Matty agrees.

Silenced by the truth, my lame defense stays lodged in my throat. Joey hasn't dropped the TRO. He knows contacting me is trouble, and he's only calling me because his girl dumped him and he wants something. How the hell did he get Matty's number? Lilliana? Maybe. I don't blame her. It's my problem, not hers. What does all this say about me, exactly? Why am I the kind of girl who would date a guy like Joey?

I can't answer that, but I should explain to the guys why Joey's calling. "It's my fault. I told him to meet me in Phoenix on the Fourth of July."

"What?! When?" Matty is incredulous.

"Relax. It was the night before we left. I couldn't sleep. I took some Benadryl. I messaged him on Facebook. It's all a blur at this point."

This last bit of information gets Spencer all excited. "Imagine if he had shown up."

"Yeah, well, that's not happening. Like Joey said, he won't be in Phoenix for the Fourth of July."

"And like I said, neither will we," Logan repeats.

"Sure we will," Spencer says. "We'll be there in an hour."

"Change of plans, bro," Logan says. "Stay on this highway through Phoenix toward Tucson. When we get to Interstate 8, we're going west."

The trip along Interstate 8 brings us through a desert of a different sort. As we approach Yuma, Arizona, and the California border, the sand changes to actual, well, sand. The white, dune kind like we have along the New Jersey shore. It's beautiful. The late afternoon sun makes me think of Christmas cards depicting the three wise men on camels, traveling along the pristine sand with a brilliant, golden star to guide their way. And then I do see the brilliant golden star, like a halo, up ahead.

"Mickey D's!" Matty shouts.

It's not the Star of Bethlehem, but after a long drive, it's practically the next-best thing.

Logan rushes us through our super-size meals. "Come on," he urges. He's piling crumpled napkins and his empty salad container on his tray. "You can eat your fries in the car. I want to cross the mountains before it gets dark."

I know what's coming next. Yep, there it is: the finger round-up motion. It hasn't made an appearance since Texas, but it's back in full force. Oh, how I've missed it.

The drive over the mountains from Yuma to San Diego is more dangerous than it looks. The mountains are steep, and there are water stations every so often—for overheated cars—along with signs reminding drivers to carry jugs of water to cool their engines while crossing these mountains and the desert.

I'm happy there's some daylight left when we cross over to the California side and drive toward San Diego. It's like the whole world springs into Technicolor. Green trees and lawns, petunias, impatiens, pretty yellow flowers I don't know the name of. Ruddy earth tones had dominated so much of our trip since Texas. It makes the contrast more spectacular. Like that first taste of sugar after you've been on a diet.

It's getting late, but Logan drives until we reach Mission Beach. After we park, I'm the first one out of the car. Matty is right behind me. We both kick off our shoes as soon as our feet touch sand. I look at Matty and don't even have to say it. We both take off running, like Dorothy and the Scarecrow through the poppy field. I know he'll get there before me. In a pool, I have a chance, but on land, there's no way I'll catch him.

I pull off my top at the edge of the dry sand but don't bother with my shorts before I dive in. I've lost count of how many times in my life I've run into crashing waves, but tonight is different. This is the Pacific Ocean. I've just driven across the entire country.

I stand with my back to the waves and look toward the shore, beyond Logan and Spencer, the parking lot, the car, the road. I inhale deeply, and it's like I can feel the distance, every single mile I traveled from New Jersey to this point, right here. The cold water doesn't bother me. I close my eyes and savor the smell of the ocean, the quiet in my mind, the intensity of the moment. When I open them again, the world snaps back into focus. I hear the sound of the waves, and Matty's laughter, right before he grabs my shoulders and pushes me under.

I lick the salt water off my lips as I sit, wrapped in a towel, on the hood of the Taurus watching the ocean and listening to the whoosh of the surf. Even though my bathing suit and shorts are still wet, inside I am warm.

"Wait until tomorrow, Rosie," Spencer says. "You'll see how blue it is."

"Are you dissing the East Coast?" I ask.

"Not at all. But the Atlantic is green. This is the Pacific. We're talking blue, blue. You'll see," Spencer says.

"So, I guess you guys have been to California before?"

"We drove the coastal highway from San Francisco to San Diego. I was eight and Logan was ten." Spencer pauses. "Our family was more of a family back then."

"Let's find someplace to stay," Logan interjects, before Spencer travels too far down memory lane.

"Thank you," I say when my eyes meet Logan's.

"You're buying your own boogie board tomorrow, Catalano," Logan says. "And don't get my car seats wet."

He turns toward the driver's door and is about to put his index finger in the air when I gently grab his wrist with one hand and push his finger down with the other. "It's okay. We're right behind you."

The Fourth of July. We're walking back to the hotel after watching the fireworks over Mission Bay when we pass a restaurant with an outdoor café. There's a small stage beyond the bar, and a band is doing a sound check. I look at the poster draped behind the drum kit. It's a sun symbol—the same one that's on the necklace from my cowboy.

"Hey, I think that's the band Lucca was talking about! Holy crap. What are the chances? We've got to check them out," I say. I don't want tonight to end. It's my last night away and our last night all together, if not forever, then for a long time.

"What kind of music do they play?" Spencer asks.

"No clue."

"Who cares?" Matty says. "It beats hanging around the hotel. Who knows when I'll ever be in San Diego again, or anywhere else for that matter."

As Logan and Spencer walk toward the outdoor café, I stop Matty and throw my arms around his middle. It takes him a moment to recover from my spontaneous display of affection before he hugs me back.

"Uh, Rosie? What's this for?"

"Everything," I say into his shirt.

"Are we done now?"

I pull away and look up at him. "Yeah. I think we're good."

I'm pleasantly surprised that the band plays a mixture of power pop and rock—Bruce-like storytelling with smart-ass, Weezer-type lyrics. Matty and Spencer, the music snobs, stand close to the stage to judge "the chops" of the band, as they put it. I sit on a bar stool, sipping a Diet Coke and accepting the ebb and flow of euphoria and melancholy as both emotions wash over me. Logan sits next to me, and I'm slightly irritated by this girl in a bikini top who's talking to him while she waits for her drink, but I watch the band and revel in the fact that I don't really want to talk to anyone at the moment. I don't have a phone anymore, but even if I did, I don't want to reach out to anyone on the "outside" right now. Tonight belongs to me and my guys.

I finish my drink, and since Logan is still yapping to this girl about ASU, I make my way toward the stage to hang with Spencer and Matty. As I squish through the crowd, the band launches into a power ballad, evoking a few whoops and some applause from fans obviously familiar with their music. I'm eyeing up my next move to cut through the throng of people when I feel hands on my hips. I hope to God it's someone I know. I gingerly turn sideways. Logan. Phew. Or maybe not. He presses against my back and sways me slowly back and forth to the music, dancing, but not really dancing. Goose bumps spread from the back of my neck across every inch of my skin. He gently lowers his chin onto the top of my head and wraps one arm across the front of me while keeping his other hand on my hip. I rest my cheek on his forearm and inhale the scent of his cologne, the scent of him. As we sway back and forth to the music, it takes every ounce of self-control I have to not turn around, put my hands on his shoulders, and—

Logan moves his lips to my ear. "I want to do so much more than kiss you, Rosie."

I know what he means. My own x-rated thoughts start with a kiss, then progress to me running my hands under his shirt and down toward the button of his jeans. I spin around and touch the tip of my nose to his. Our lips are about a centimeter apart. Either I stop right now or not at all.

"What are you thinking?" I ask.

"That I'm going to be in Arizona and, after tomorrow, you're not. You?"

"I'm thinking about something Avery said and . . . I've still got a lot of things I need to work out." I stand on my tiptoes. This time I'm the one whispering in his ear. "To be continued," I say. "I hope."

When I pull back, he looks confused or hurt or both. But he doesn't press me. Unlike Joey, Logan is not the kind of guy who would start something he couldn't finish, and maybe for the first time ever, neither am I. When the song ends, so does our moment. Sometimes, it really is best to do nothing.

Chapter 18

For as long as I can remember, our family has been renting the same beach house at the New Jersey shore. Rentals begin and end on Saturdays, with the standard "checkout" time being eleven in the morning. It doesn't matter if we're there for a week or a month, come Saturday, no one ever wants to leave. So every year, for as long as I can remember, we kid ourselves. We say: "Even though we have to be out of the house by eleven, we can still spend the rest of the day on the beach. Right?" But guess what? That never happens. Because once we've packed the car with bedding to boogie boards and vacuumed up sand from the hardwood floors, the vacation is over. Stretching it a few more hours wouldn't feel right. Our time at the beach ends when we turn in our key.

That's how I feel when we arrive in Tempe on Sunday. We're taking a red-eye home, so we still have the entire day to look around, check out the ASU campus and Logan's dorm, and grab some dinner. But the collective mood of our little foursome makes me realize our road trip ended when we crossed the mountains, out of California back into Arizona.

It's nearly dark when Logan pulls up curbside at Sky Harbor Airport. On the ride over, I obsessed about how I was going to say good-bye. Should I kiss him on the cheek? Tell him I'll call him when I get home? Ask him when we'll see each other again? In the end, it turns out to be none of the above. Logan gets out of the driver's seat, walks around the back, and pops the trunk. I stand on the sidewalk, fiddling with my hair, as he helps the boys unload our bags before shaking Matty's hand and giving Spencer a brotherly hug. Then he turns to me, opens his arms to bear-hug width, and says, "Rosie." I step toward him and give him an awkward squeeze with my backpack slung over one shoulder. When I look into his eyes, I want to cry. I get it; there's too much to say, so we aren't saying anything. Almost. I do, however, manage to whisper, "Thanks for the ride."

Twenty-five minutes later, we've made it through

security and I'm standing at a newsstand, deciding on snacks and reading material for the five-hour plane ride home. It's an overnight flight, but I know I'm not going to be able to sleep. I push away the image of Logan pulling away from the curb in the Taurus and the overwhelming sensation that my home for the past nine days has left me. I shake it off. I have to. This trip put me back together, and I refuse to get all torn apart again. So there, Logan Davidson. Enjoy your 120-degree Rosie-free Arizona summer. I'm just about to reach for one of the magazines listing the one hundred best college deals when Matty practically tackles me and pulls me into the aisle with the paperbacks.

"Get your hands off me, you big goon," I say. By now, he knows I mean "big goon" in the best-possible way.

"Joey's here," Spencer says.

"Oh, *Dios mío!*" Apparently emergencies turn me into my mother. "How can that be? He said he wasn't coming."

"He lied," Matty says. "Big surprise."

"Okay, here's what we're going to do. Spencer, follow him and try to find out what flight he's on. If he's on our plane, we'll simply change our tickets and take the next flight home. No need to panic, right?" I take a deep breath. "Spencer, what are you doing? Get going."

Spencer shrugs. "He's not here." Then he high-fives Matty, who's all pressed up against the bestsellers with me.

Matty grins, releasing me. "I couldn't resist."

I expel all the air from my lungs and am reminded of Batman dive bombing my hair at the caverns—too relieved to even be angry. "Come on. We'd better get to our gate."

Matty raises his eyebrows. "That's it?" He sounds disappointed.

"Not exactly the reaction we were going for," Spencer agrees.

"Maybe it's time you started expecting the unexpected. At least where I'm concerned," I say.

On the plane, Matty, Spence, and I sit three across in an emergency exit row, the kind with all the extra leg room. Sweet karma. I remember why Spencer wanted Matty along to begin with and I offer to hold his hand during takeoff.

"It's okay, Rosie. I don't think I'm afraid to fly anymore."

I grab his and Matty's hands anyway. *Neither am I,* I think.

The flight seems excruciatingly long, and when they finally allow us to deplane, I want to sprint down the aisle, which, of course, isn't possible. Instead, I watch the other passengers search through the overhead bins and wait as one row of people at a time make their way toward the exit.

Inside the terminal, we head for baggage claim on the lower level. I stand by the automatic doors while Matty and Spencer go and pick up our luggage and Spencer's guitar, which required special cargo instructions. I keep peeking through the doors to see if I can spot my dad's car. Outside, the sun is rising. I'm considering waiting by the curb and trusting Matty and Spencer will know where to find me when I see the boys coming toward me with all our bags and the guitar. Hooray for me, positive energy continues. Except—"That's not my bag." My heart sinks. My favorite sandals are in there. And the dress I wore the night we all went out in Dallas, and the Elvis stuff for my family, and the necklace from my cowboy. What if somebody took my bag by mistake?

"Stay right here," I say, grabbing my suitcase's doppelgänger from Matty. "I'll find it."

"We'll go back," Matty offers.

"It's okay, really." Matty's handled too much for me already. "I'll be quick. See if you can spot my dad."

I dash back to the baggage carousel. I don't want the person whose luggage got switched with mine to leave. I arrive at carousel 2, which only has a few bags left, including mine.

I see it turning the bend on the conveyor belt. As fast as I can, I throw the strange bag back and head for mine. *Come to Mama.* I'm jogging alongside my suitcase and am about to snatch it before it goes around another turn when I hear—

"Rosie!"

Joey.

Slowly, I turn as my bag continues along on its merry way.

He's on the other side of the carousel and partially blocked from view by the chute where the bags come out.

"What are you doing here?" I look back over my shoulder to see if I can spot Matty or Spencer. I feel trapped.

"I've been trying to talk to you."

Me and my big mouth. Why'd I go and tell him I'd be on the red-eye today? I keep moving along the belt. I just want to get my bag and sprint toward the door. Joey follows my gaze and grabs my suitcase before I can.

"Drop the suitcase, Joey," I say. I don't want to get any closer. I'm probably already within TRO violation territory. "You know I can't talk to you. Whatever you need to say, tell it to my lawyer."

"Come on, Rosie. I miss you."

He's lying. I know it. He's up to something; I just don't know what it is.

"Maybe we can work things out without going to court."

Hmm. Why does Joey want to stay out of court? "So drop the TRO, why don't you," I snap. "You're the one who filed for court protection from big, bad Rosie."

I want my suitcase. I'm not going to lose all my special memories because of Joey. I take a few steps backward, keeping Joey in sight while glancing around for any sign of Matty and Spencer. Joey starts moving toward me. "Come on, Rosie. Let me hand this to you."

"Just leave it right there, Joey. You're going to get me in more trouble."

The internal struggle is becoming too much. I'm about to say screw it and just get the hell out of there when, out of nowhere, Spencer comes up behind Joey and screams: "Drop the bag."

Startled, Joey whips his head around and that's when it happens, Bam! His face smashes into the guitar case Spencer has slung over his shoulder. I didn't think Joey hit it that hard, but he obviously hit it the wrong way because blood spurts everywhere. Holy mother of God! I'm ashamed to admit this, but my first reaction is to run toward Joey so I can grab my suitcase and sprint for the exit.

And that's exactly what I do.

Chapter 19

So much can happen in nine days. I sit on my bed, laptop on my knees, paging through all the photos from our trip. Matty brought them over on a flash drive this morning. He probably could've just e-mailed them, but he said he also wanted to wish me luck. Me and my parents are meeting with Steve Justice later today. Anyway, I'm glad he stopped by.

It's so weird, I think as the photos slide by. During the school year, the weeks can sometimes blur together like one colorless, uneventful day. But in just over a week, I'd been from Chestnutville, New Jersey, to the Pacific Ocean and back again: 3,165 miles of driving. Spencer tracked it.

I thought it would feel good to wake up in my own bed this morning, but honestly, it was strange. Despite the fact that Pony was plastered against me, his head on my pillow with one paw draped over my shoulder, I felt lonely.

Yesterday morning, after I recovered from my initial reaction to the Joey bloodbath at Newark Liberty Airport, I returned to carousel 2 with my dad to find Spencer, Matty, and Joey's brother all gathered around him. Spencer, who of course is certified in CPR and first aid, was applying a makeshift compress to Joey's nose. It looked like someone's T-shirt, but I really didn't want to ask. I just stood beside my dad until airport security arrived with one of those golf-cart-type vehicles to help Joey to his brother's car. All this time I wondered how it would feel to talk to Joey again, but as I watched him drive away, I didn't feel love or like or even hate. All I felt was sorry. For everything.

When Miranda called early this morning to confirm our meeting, she said she heard from Joey's counsel that his nose is, in fact, broken. But technically, since it was no one's fault, no one is in trouble. Yet. My court date is Thursday, so we'll see.

I called Avery last night to fill her in on everything from San Diego to the guitar-case attack on Joey's nose. I also wanted to run an idea by her. Regardless of what happens Thursday, I know I've got a karmic debt to repay (seeing my dad's shocked, pale face at the airport when he saw Joey's nose really brought that point home), and I've got a two-part plan for how to do it. Avery loved what I came up with, and she even offered to fly in for my court appearance. It was sweet of her to offer, but I didn't want her to spend that kind of money. She just laughed and said, "In case you haven't noticed, my family is loaded." I told her to save the trip to New Jersey for a happier occasion.

Mom knocks on my door just as I click on a photo of me and Logan—the one Matty took of the two of us sitting on the edge of the Grand Canyon.

"Come in," I say.

She comes over to my bed and peers at the screen. I consider closing the photo before she sits down but don't.

"Nice picture," she says. It is.

I can tell she's worried that I've fallen crazy in love again. I haven't. Even if I had, I'm determined not to contact Logan until I work out some things or he contacts me, whichever comes first. In the words of both Spencer and Yoda, "Stalk no more, I will not."

I push my laptop aside and throw my arms around my

mom. She's nothing short of stunned. "I'm so sorry, Mom. For everything I put you and Dad through."

"Sweetheart, it's okay. We love you . . . just don't do it again."

She laughs, but I know she means it. If she didn't see my hug coming, this is going to knock her flip-flops off.

"Mom?"

"Yes?"

"I think I might like to go into fashion design. I'm going to take drawing as my elective this year, and I want to learn how to sew."

"I think that's a great idea, *mija*," Mom says. "Abuelita would love to show you, and you know your father has some machines at the factory, for small detail work. You can practice there."

Now I'm the one who's shocked. "I thought you would laugh at me."

Mom puts her hands on my shoulders and leans back to look at me. "What? You don't think I remember Rosie Couture?"

I tilt my head and smile. "You were my best client."

"And biggest fan." Mom cups my face in her hands like I'm six again.

"Well, as long as that didn't surprise you, I've got something else I want to talk to you about." This time I put my hands on her shoulders.

"I'm listening."

"It can wait until after we see Steve Justice today. I want Dad to be there too."

She kisses the top of my head. "More coffee?"

"Definitely."

"I'll put a pot on. Meet me in the kitchen."

"I'm going to be better, Mom. Wait and see."

"We don't want you to be better, Rosie. Just happy."

Steve Justice opens a bottle of Tums and shakes four into his palm. He's a thin guy, fortyish, with a friendly, elflike face. He started off all smiles, but I think I'm giving him agita. I've just finished running down the chain of events leading up to Joey's arrival at the airport and Spencer's guitar accidentally breaking my ex's nose. Poor Steve. I'm too much for him. I wonder if this will cost my dad more money.

Miranda is seated at the conference table with us in Steve's office. She's younger than I thought she'd be, early twenties maybe, with greenish-blue eyes and pretty auburn hair that she's wearing in a neat French braid.

"The good news is," Miranda says, "we've found an eye-witness. The neighbor I told you about? Lucky for us, she's a big fan of the *Late Late Show*. She saw Joey on the night of the fire."

Miranda goes on to explain that the neighbor watched Joey walk over to the burning box and attempt to snuff out the fire with his baseball cap. According to the neighbor, when flames engulfed his cap, Joey looked panicked and flung it. She said it sailed through the open car window and landed on the driver's seat of Joey's Mustang. The faux fur seat covers ignited instantly.

"And get this," Miranda continues. "The neighbor lady said he retrieved a fire extinguisher from the house, but then, instead of using it immediately, he stood there and watched the car burn for a while. The neighbor said she was getting nervous about the flames reaching the gas tank and was about to dial 911 when he finally put the fire out."

That bastard!

"So I wasn't responsible for totaling his car. How cool is that?" I'm all excited.

"It would be a lot cooler if you hadn't also continued to stalk him," Steve says drily.

Stalk, schmalk. Joey is such a wuss. I did what most kids

my age do when they break up. It's not all that easy to let go.

"So you think Joey wanted his car totaled?" Dad asks. "Does this qualify as insurance fraud?"

"It's possible," Steve says. "We're certainly going to bring the matter up with his attorney. I have a call in to her already."

"That is awesome!" I say. "Do you think he'll drop everything?"

"Don't get too excited," Steve says. "You still might be looking at community service for the TRO violations."

I kinda figured that might be the case. That's why I came up with my two-part plan.

"I just hope they don't press any charges against Spencer. The nose wasn't his fault."

"So far, no news is good news," Miranda says.

I'm still nervous. Joey tried to pin the torched car on me, so it's possible his mommy is looking for someone to blame for breaking his nose. Especially if he needs plastic surgery.

"Now then," Steve says. "Let's talk about Thursday."

Steve reviews court procedure so I'll know what to expect, and after he answers all our questions, we say our good-byes.

"I don't know about anybody else," Dad says as we leave Steve's office, "but I could go for pizza."

Emotional eating. No mystery where I get it from.

"Let's get takeout," I say. "I've got something I want to run by you both, and I want Matty to be there."

Matty and my brother are sitting on our back deck when we pull into the driveway. I help Dad carry the food, and Mom walks toward the kitchen door.

"It's a nice night," she says. "I'll grab some paper plates and napkins and we can eat out here."

The five of us sit around the glass-top patio table, making short work of the pizzas, antipasto, and bread sticks. Pony is at my feet waiting for me to slip him my crust, and if I didn't have to make an appearance in court in thirty-six hours, all would feel right with the world.

"So, Dad," I say as we're finishing dinner and Mom breaks out the ice cream. "I've been thinking about what Steve said about community service. Maybe . . . well, could you use some help at the factory?"

My dad questions me with his eyebrows. "You're saying you want to work for me, for free? It's a nice gesture, but I don't think that counts as community service."

"No, no, this is more of an idea I had. I'd like to start a class."

"Class? What kind of class?" Dad asks.

"Not a class, really. More like a group. An English conversation group. You know, so nonnative speakers can practice their skills? I know I'm not a teacher or anything, but I'm almost bilingual. Do you think some of your employees would be interested?"

Eddie looks dumbfounded. "Hey, Matty, what'd you do with Rosie? Did you leave her in New Mexico? Nice job finding a replacement, though. Looks just like her."

Mom shakes her head at Eddie and puts her hand on mine. "That's a great idea, honey. Your grandparents would have loved to have something like that when they came here. English can be so confusing."

I nod in agreement, then stick out my tongue at Eddie, just to make sure he knows it's me and not my angelic twin. "I was thinking I could start with some practical phrases like ordering from a menu or going to the bank. Then maybe some small talk, like about celebrities and pop culture? I did a little research online. There are actually lesson plans out there, and I found out the library runs a similar eight-week course. I'm gonna stop by there tomorrow. Get some tips."

"Do you even know where the library is?" Eddie asks in fake awe.

"Enough," Dad says. "Tell you what. Put together a

plan and I'll see if anyone is interested. But it will have to be on their time. Lunch breaks or after hours."

"Got it," I say.

"Good." Dad's not letting on how proud he is that I came up with this idea, but I can see it in his eyes, and that's all that matters.

"Hey, maybe me and Spencer could help out too? We're looking for a community service project to do for our junior year," Matty says.

"That would be great, Matty," I say. "Thank you. I know I don't say it enough, but you are the best."

Matty's cheeks go red, and Mom raises her Diet Coke. "To Matty."

We all click plastic cups.

Even though I didn't get to work at the bridal shop, and the dog-walking business fell by the wayside, I'm excited about the summer that's emerging from the ashes. I wasn't always the kind of girl who wakes up early on a summer day and heads to the library to gather information on how to teach an ESL class. But tomorrow, that's exactly what I'm going to do. First, I've got explain to everyone that my plan includes a part two.

Chapter 20

Thursday, July 9. My much-dreaded court date has arrived. I'm seated in the front row of the courtroom. Steve Justice is to my right, by the aisle. Mom, Dad, Eddie, Matty, Spencer, and Lilliana are to my left—we take up the entire first row. We're turning a TRO appearance into an afternoon at the theater.

We wait for the judge to take the bench, and each time someone new comes into the courtroom, the doors swings open and bangs dramatically against the wall. They could really use a stopper or a heavier door.

Aside from rattling my nerves, the noise also makes me glance nervously over my shoulder to see who's arriving. Part of me hopes I won't see Joey or anyone in his family (so far, so good), and part of me keeps expecting Logan, although I don't know why. We just left him in Arizona. Plane tickets are expensive, and his classes have started. I know Spencer has been in touch with his brother about the whole "airport incident," but I haven't heard a word from him. Not one. Granted, I haven't gotten a new cell phone yet, but he's a smart guy; if he wanted to reach me, he could. It's okay, though. I didn't have time this week to let it bother me. I spent most of yesterday working on my lesson plans.

Finally, the judge enters the courtroom and we all stand.

"Please be seated," she says. She puts on her reading glasses and opens a file. I'm not the only one in court today: There are numerous traffic violations and another TRO appearance, which is the first case on the docket. When the judge calls the defendant in that case, the complaining witness decides to drop the allegations, saying she was mistaken when she said her husband had hit her and threatened to kill her. I'm afraid for her. The judge looks doubtful and disappointed but adjourns the case nonetheless. After sitting through appearances on DUIs, speeding tickets, and parking violations, it's finally my turn.

My underarms are sweaty and I can feel the redness starting in my face and spreading all over my body as the bailiff announces my case. *State of New Jersey v. Rosalita*

Ariana Catalano. The judge is the first to speak.

"We are here today to decide if this temporary restraining order will become permanent. The defendant, Ms. Catalano, will have a chance to dispute the allegations. After that, I will make my decision. I've read your evidence in this case, Mr. Justice," Judge Tomlinson says. "I understand you're prepared to call a witness."

"Yes, Your Honor, we are."

I turn around and see Joey's elderly neighbor in the back row. She's all dressed up and rocking a nice shade of pink lipstick. She waves at Steve when he glances her way.

I'm relieved Joey and his parents didn't show. Steve explained beforehand that they weren't required to be here. Joey's probably not making any public appearances until his nose heals. No one ever said he wasn't vain.

Anyway, this is my day in court, an opportunity for me to answer the allegations in the temporary restraining order. I hope the judge appreciates my honesty and sincerity and goes easy on me. I don't know what I'll do if the temporary order becomes permanent. Staying away from Joey won't be the hard part, since we go to different schools, but it might get awkward for Eddie, Matty, and Spencer. Come September, they'll see Joey every day. Not to mention, being a girl under a restraining order won't garner me any votes for prom queen this year. I'll be lucky to get a date.

"Well, then, Mr. Justice," the judge says. "Shall we hear from your witness?"

That's when the prosecutor, an attractive older woman, stands up.

My palms are sweating and my entire body feels hot as I stare at the judge and wonder how this is all going to play out. I'm on the edge of losing it when the prosecutor speaks. "Your Honor, that won't be necessary. We have approved a request made by Mr. Marconi's attorney that the allegations against Ms. Catalano be dropped."

At that moment, it seems like my entire row lets out a collective sigh of relief. I turn to Steve, who's grinning big, like the Cheshire cat. I have the urge to high-five him, but I keep my glee in check.

This is exactly what we were hoping for! Steve contacted Joey's attorney and informed her that he was reaching out to the insurance company responsible for paying the claim submitted by Joey's parents for the totaled car. Steve also said once our eyewitness had testified, he would make the claims adjuster aware of her testimony as well. If Joey's

JENNIFER SALVATO DOKTORSKI

mom had been attempting to commit fraud, Steve figured that would be enough to make them drop their petition for a permanent restraining order, and Steve was right.

The courtroom goes quiet again as the judge is about to speak. "Well, then, as much as I'd like to adjourn this case and grab an early lunch today, I for one am not willing to excuse Ms. Catalano's clear violations of the TRO while it was in place. Violations, I might add, that Mr. Marconi made the court aware of through counsel." She's looking at Joey's attorney when she says that last part.

The judge picks up a piece of paper and reads. "Let's see, two text messages, one message through a social networking website, a phone conversation between Mr. Marconi and an unnamed associate of Ms. Catalano, and, the granddaddy of them all, Ms. Catalano's violation of space restrictions at Newark Liberty Airport on July sixth."

Huh? The granddaddy of them all? I came to court today completely prepared to pay for my mistakes. I never wanted to weasel out of my TRO violations, and I can accept my much-deserved punishment for the things I did wrong, but that last one's not fair. Joey was the one who came to meet *me*. I'm squirming in my seat, itching to say something, but Steve shoots me a look that says: *Zip it*. At least the judge didn't mention Joey's broken nose. I guess he's not blaming me for that, too. Again, this speaks to Joey's vanity, not his sense of decency. How would it look if people found out that Spencer's guitar case had kicked Joey's ass? Or, in this instance, face.

The courtroom door swings open again with a bang. I hold my breath and close my eyes as I prepare to turn around and see who walked in. I'm convinced it's Joey or his parents.

"Avery!" Matty yelps.

She flutters in like Tinkerbell, looks at the judge, and gives her a smile and small wave. "Sorry, ma'am," she says with her cute Texas accent, then scurries up the aisle and sits in the second row, right behind me. My throat feels tight. I turn and mouth, *Thank you*. Avery gives me a thumbs-up. After I told her it wasn't necessary to come today, I didn't expect her to show up! I may have lost Joey and some self-respect, but I made three new friends—great friends—as a result of this whole mess. I'm including Logan in that count even though I'm not sure where we stand.

"Mr. Justice," Judge Tomlison says, "would you like to address your client's alleged violations of the TRO?"

I'm not happy that Joey showing up at the airport got lumped in there, but I'm prepared to accept my punishment. I told Steve I didn't want to make any excuses. All my friends and family have been ridiculously supportive even when I haven't deserved it. I owe it to myself to face what I did, admit I was wrong, and recover my dignity. Not only that, but I feel I owe it to the universe. People have given me so much these last few weeks, and I've got to start giving back—and I mean by doing more than court-ordered community service.

In fact, I'm starting this afternoon. My hair is all washed and pulled back in a neat ponytail, not only because it's a conservative look for my court appearance, but because I'm going to see my hairstylist, Jimmi Gerard, so we can chop my hair off into a nice bob with a wedge and donate my hair to Locks of Love for kids with cancer. It's not saving the world or anything, but anyone who knows me knows it's a sacrifice. One small step for Rosie.

Steve answers the judge's question about my TRO violations. "That won't be necessary, Your Honor. Ms. Catalano is not contesting those allegations."

Judge Tomlinson writes something down and shuffles some pages before speaking again. "Okay, then, that will conclude your appearance on the TRO today, Ms. Catalano. We will set a date for your sentencing, and at that time I will determine how you will make amends for your transgressions. But let me say this: I do not appreciate your taking that TRO lightly, and I would anticipate probation and some community service in your future," she says. "Being named in a TRO at the tender age of seventeen is nothing to be proud of, and I intend to make sure you learn a lesson. After your sentencing, I do not want to see you in my court again. Is that understood?"

"Yes, Your Honor. It is," I say.

Then I lean over and whisper in Steve's ear, reminding him about my two-part plan. I discussed it with him when we arrived at the courthouse this morning.

He clears his throat. "Your Honor, if I may. My client and I are wondering if that anticipated community service needs to be served in its entirety within Essex County and, more exactly, New Jersey."

The judge raises her eyebrows. "Approach the bench, Mr. Justice."

I clench my fists in anticipation as Steve converses with the judge in hushed tones.

"In August?!" the judge exclaims. "It's going to be hotter than Hades." Then she looks over at me and I give her a sheepish grin. "I like it!" she says. "I think it will be a good experience for Ms. Catalano."

When I turn around to face Avery, she's all smiles.

Chapter 21

The Texas sun beats down on me, causing sweat to pour down the entire length of my face, starting above my hairline, somewhere under my white hard hat. The top of my head is easily ten degrees hotter than the rest of my body.

The coordinators for Habitat for Humanity have had a radio playing all morning, but it's hard to hear over the staccato hammering and the constant buzz of power saws and drills. Anyway, this close to the Mexican border, the musical options seem limited to country and Tejano. I'm still wearing goggles from a morning holding the ends of two-by-fours while one of the supervisors ran them through a circular saw. My face may feel cooler if I take them off, but judging from the white paint speckles, I'm doing a service to my eyes while painting this six-foot fence at one of the nearly completed homes. El Paso in August. There's nothing like it.

"What kind of guitar did you wind up getting Matty?" Avery is painting alongside me.

"A Yamaha. I went for the more expensive model, even though Matty said I didn't have to. He deserves it."

"What about your class? Are y'all gonna keep teaching it in the fall?"

"Yeah, about that. It didn't exactly turn out to be my class. My neighbor, Mrs. Friedman, is a retired English teacher. She wound up running the class while Matty, Spence, and I helped out."

"Still, it was your idea," she says. "You should feel proud."

"I do, but with Mrs. Friedman doing most of the work, I wanted to find some other way to serve the New Jersey part of my community service. Mrs. Friedman helped with that, too. She got me a gig doing makeovers at the senior center."

Avery laughs. "Sounds like a better match for your skill set."

"Hey, I'm good. Those older gals looked ten years younger when I was done with them!"

This summer has been super busy. I've learned that hard work sure does keep a girl out of trouble. In addition to the English conversation class, my dad wound up employing me, Matty, and Spencer at the lampshade factory. I worked in the office, and my dad taught the guys to run the stitching and cutting machines. I used my lunch hour to practice sewing. I even made two sundresses, designed entirely by yours truly. The boys are still working at the factory and will be until Labor Day. I'll be here in Texas until then, building houses with Avery and paying off the balance on my debt to society. The New Jersey chapter of Habitat for Humanity would have been happy to have me, but it's nice to be able to experience this with a friend.

"I sure wish we were on that beach of yours right now," Avery says.

"Tell me about it."

My vacation at Lilliana's family beach house never happened. I was too busy. But after surprising me in court that day, Avery stayed in New Jersey for a week and we took some day trips to the beach. It was a blast. She got along fabulously with Lilliana and Marissa, and us girls hung out with Matty and Spencer the entire time. It was more fun than I deserved to have. By the end of the week, it was clear that Avery and Matty are into each other, but who knows if anything will ever come of that. Like Avery said, time and distance (not to mention age) are not in their favor now. Still, life's all about the possibilities.

Avery and I have been painting this fence for an hour now. I cannot wait until it's time to break for lunch. I look like crap. I'm not wearing any makeup, my short hair is no doubt a matted mess under this hard hat, and my white Habitat for Humanity T-shirt is soaked through around my neck, down my back, and under my armpits.

"Have you heard from him?" she asks. This is the first time Avery's mentioned Logan. I clutch my paintbrush tighter.

"No. But I'm sure he's real busy sustaining things," I say. Too bad one of those things wasn't a connection with me. I'm so stupid. I thought we'd at least come out of all this friends. *Live and learn, Rosie.* It's time to work on me.

I'm proud of the steps I've been taking. I've been gathering college applications, and my parents said they'll take me to visit FIT in September. I'm even trying to talk them into letting me go to public school this fall—to save on my Catholic school tuition—but they don't think it's a good idea for me and Joey to be in the same building, even though I know I can handle it. It's just as well; I'd miss being with Lilliana and Marissa, but somehow, if I wind up staying at Sacred Heart, I'm going to miss Matty more. I've grown majorly attached to him this summer. Not in a boyfriend-girlfriend way. It's more about sharing an experience that only the two of us, and Spencer and Logan of course, can understand.

I think back to my first day home. I felt so lost in my own town. The houses were all so much smaller and closer together than I remembered. And there was the traffic and the crowds; there was no breathing room. That's the way it is, living in a suburb so close to New York City, but after my road trip, nothing felt right. Nothing felt the same. I know Matty felt it too. Still does. He would have given anything to come here with me to build houses, see Avery, look up at the big night sky.

Avery bends down and uses a screwdriver to pry open another can of paint.

"So, do you think you're gonna call him?"

"Call who?" I play dumb.

She sighs. "Logan."

"Logan? Why on earth would I want to call Logan?" It comes out much louder and angrier than I expect.

"Because you haven't spoken to him in over a month," a familiar male voice says from behind me. I drop my paintbrush on my work boot.

Logan.

He's standing about ten feet away from me, wearing a hard hat, a Habitat T-shirt, and jeans that are baggier than I'm used to seeing on him, but that doesn't stop him from looking good. Slowly, I walk toward him until I'm right up in his face—eyeball to plastic goggles. I want to make sure I'm not imagining this.

"What are you doing here?" I say softly.

"Building houses, what else?"

"You drove six hours in that blasted maroon Taurus to build houses?"

He doesn't ask how I know it's six hours from Tempe to El Paso and I don't ask him if there's a local chapter of Habitat for Humanity in Tempe. Instead, we stare at each other. He reaches over and takes off my goggles and lets them drop to the ground. Then he grabs my hips, pulls me close, and kisses me.

We only separate when one of the supervisors whistles loudly at us through his teeth. "This isn't a high school dance," he says.

"He's right," I say. "I've still got a lot of work to do." I pick up my goggles and walk toward my unfinished fence and Avery, who's pretending she's been painting this whole time. I glance over my shoulder, raise my index finger in the air, and make a lasso motion.

I turn back toward the fence and smile when I hear Logan jogging toward me.

Acknowledgments

It's difficult to express the deep sense of gratitude
I feel for all those who helped make my dream a reality, but
I will try my best to name everyone before the music is cued
up and I'm ushered off the stage.

Thanks to Kerry Sparks, my amazing agent, for res-
cuing me from the slush pile, believing in my writing,
and working so hard to make me a published author. You
rock!

To my editor extraordinaire, Annette Pollert, for her
unwavering enthusiasm in championing and editing this
novel. Thank you for making every sentence, on every page,
better and for understanding Rosie's charms and a cowboy's
allure. I am so lucky to have had the opportunity to work
with you!

And to all the amazing people at Simon Pulse, especially Bethany Buck, Mara Anastas, Katherine Devendorf, Karina Granda, Carolyn Swerdloff, Siena Koncsol, Karen Taschek, and Lara Stelmaszyk.

To Sarah Cloots and Rekha Radhakrishnan, editorial consultants, for reading early drafts of this novel and providing the perfect road map for revision.

To the Rutgers Council on Children's Literature and the New Jersey chapter of SCBWI, for providing writers with the opportunity to make connections and perfect their craft.

To my writer friends who so generously give of their time and talents and push me to become a better writer: Melissa Eisen Azarian, L. P. Chase, Karen Cleveland, James Gelsey, Sharon Biggs Waller, and especially Lisa Anne Reiss, without whom I never would have finished that very first draft. I am blessed to have you all in my corner.

To Jorge Miranda and Magaly Barzola, for their excellent Spanish translation. Thank you.

To Michael Justice, Esq., for his legal advice and humor, both of which made this novel better.

To my book clubbers, Sheryl Citro, Jen Post, Lori Mido, and Francine Ruzich, for reading my drafts and listening patiently as I shared each milestone on the road to publication.

To my *comadre*, Adriana Calderon, for believing in me when I sent that first query letter to *Cosmo* all those years ago and for reading more drafts of my work than anyone should ever have to. And to her husband, Steven O'Donnell.

To my wonderful friends, for years of antics, adventures, and road trips—the kind worth writing about!—Diana and Joe Barbour, Jeff Davis, Jennifer Johnston, Esther Northrup, Lisa Paccio, Dean Potter, and Tracy Sharkey.

To my grandmothers, Theresa Juliano and Columbia Salvato, for their respective love of words and storytelling, and to my grandfathers, James Juliano and George Salvato, my first fans.

To Dolores and John Doktorski, who make me feel like their daughter.

To my sister, Melissa Collucci, for always being the voice that tells me I can, especially when the one inside says I can't. And to her family, Anthony (more brother than in-law), Anthony James, and Cassie. I love you all.

Most important, I must thank the other two-thirds of my power trio, who put up with me on a daily basis.

To my husband, Mike Doktorski, without whose constant love, support, understanding, and patience (lots and *lots* of patience), I'd be lost, and to our daughter, Carley—our greatest gift—who, when she was only six years old, said to me upon my completion of the first draft of my first novel: "Mommy, even if no one buys your book, you're still an author." God bless her. Thank you for allowing me the time and space to pursue my dreams. I love you both so much!

Finally, to the Power Trio I give thanks to every day for all that is good.

About the Author

JENNIFER SALVATO DOKTORSKI once took a cross-country road trip in a celery-green Oldsmobile. She's a freelance writer who has written articles and essays for national publications, including *Cosmopolitan*. She lives in New Jersey with her family and their dog, Buffy (The Squeaky Toy Slayer). *How My Summer Went Up in Flames* is her debut novel. Visit her at jendoktorski.com.

Feisty. Flirty. Fun. Fantastic.

LAUREN BARNHOLDT

siMonTeeN

Simon & Schuster's **Simon Teen**
e-newsletter delivers current updates on
the hottest titles, exciting sweepstakes, and
exclusive content from your favorite authors.

Visit **TEEN.SimonandSchuster.com** to
sign up, post your thoughts, and find out what
every avid reader is talking about!

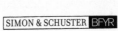